A JOURNEY THROUGH BLACK FOREST, PALACES, AND MUSEUMS IN THE DEUTSCHLAND

GERMANY

Dr Shrikant Watawe

DEDICATION

This book is dedicated to the persons who have imbibed in themselves the attitude to travel, enjoy and write their experiences which visualize the importance of traveling. It is a result of self-experience and exploration which we continue doing in our life. It should be able to help tourists to enjoy the places mentioned in the book when they visit them. Even though Germany with its palaces, modernization and the forests is a favourite tourism destination across the world, exploring it differently requires a different view. The book is, therefore, a testimony to our self-planned German travel and is narrated simply with a lot of pictures and personal experiences. This small handy book is expected to be a suitable guide for the tourist when visiting the places mentioned in it. However, we fell short of time in some places we had ample of free time otherwise to experience the different cities. We are sure that this book will do justice to these cities from a tourist's viewpoint. The photographs included in the book are our sole property and if any person happens to be included in any of the photographs, it is purely coincidental, unintentional, and attributable to the situation at that time. We also thank persons who willingly allowed us to take their photos during their festival season.

ACKNOWLEDGEMENTS

It is a great pleasure to thank all the people who were involved in the planning and execution of our German tour. The planning of the tour had started at home months ago but it materialized after an elaborate discussion with Mrs Shruti Kuber who was in Pune during December 2023. With extensive discussions regarding the destinations, places to see, and most importantly travel, she guided us with the 49-euro monthly pass which was highly economical and very easy to use. We could use it for all modes of transport in any German city. We could not use it for the IC or ICE superfast trains. This did not hamper our travel in any way. Then visits to some places which are not easily accessible as the travel destinations were also discussed. My spouse Mrs. Shraddha, being a good financial planner, made it a financially successful and manageable trip and I am also thankful to her. There were suggestions and advice from Mr Datta Deshpande to make this write-up more meaningful and simpler. He has made an immense contribution to editing the book and making it more readable. Mr. Ratnadeep Todkar, from Samarth Holidays Kolhapur, helped us to plan meticulously. He has always been responsible for our successful and enjoyable touring experience. I must also thank all the persons who are directly or indirectly responsible for the completion and publication of this book.

INDEX

Sl. No.	Title	Page Number
1	Things to carry while on tour	5
2	The Planning	6
3	The Travel Plan	7
4	Frankfurt and Rudrashem	13
5	Stuttgart	18
6	Munich	32
7	Nurenburg	46
8	Leipzig	51
9	Berlin	55
10	Hamburg	71
11	Cologne	78
12	Frankfurt	87

THINGS TO CARRY WHILE ON TOUR

There are many aspects to what to carry and what not to. Some travellers like to carry heavy luggage, which includes a lot of stuff, specifically clothes, and food items. For them, it is almost a dress a day, which makes the luggage very bulky, heavy, and at times difficult to carry. When making an effort to minimize the luggage it is pertinent to carry the most essential things, which are again person-specific and destination-specific. For those traveling on their own, i.e. without being part of a group tour, and preferring Indian food, here is a note of caution. Ready-to-eat packets, though helpful, increase the luggage weight. The young may prefer backpacks and carry very little things but this could only be suitable for a short duration. In our case, no doubt we prefer vegan food but we can manage with a few items from non-vegetarian food. Besides we mostly prefer the local food of the place we visit as it is fresh and readily available. Tasting the local food, especially the local street food, is always an enjoyable experience. Since our total tour period was 21 days we needed to carry enough clothes keeping in mind the fact that the average temperature there even during the summers is around 18 to 20 degrees Celsius. Certainly, sweaters, warm clothing, rain jackets, caps, umbrellas, sunglasses, a good pair of shoes, a sufficient quantity of socks, and floaters are necessary. Most importantly the documents that should always be carried are the Passport (original) & VISA form/documents/photos, Insurance papers (original), FOREX receipts, and Custom declaration form, if more than one Camera/lens is to be carried, Driving license (original), Tickets (Air, Train, Parks etc.), Forex card, Debit/Credit card, Emergency contact numbers sheet, Travel itinerary + maps, a notepad and pen. In electronics we require a Camera + chargers for the camera and mobile + memory cards, Mobile having GPS navigation system and a Universal adapter for all electronic gadgets. A small coffee maker or a Heating coil, if the place of stay does not have this facility, toothpaste, and a toothbrush are also a must. The other things that are required are Deodorant, Sunscreen cream, Shaving cream, razor, Talcum powder, Disposable soap stripes, Hair oil a small 50 ml bottle, Mosquito repellent, Binoculars, Spare locks for bags, Ear plugs (for airplane travel), Neck pillow (for airplane travel), Medicines with Doctor's prescriptions, Band-Aid stripes, Kailas Jivan, Vicks, a knife, a small torch, safety pins and plastic bags. Some of the things mentioned here may be destination-specific. The bags should be of a suitable size to fit in all the material properly and also have a little free space to accommodate items purchased during the tour. One handbag or sac which would hold all important documents and be with you all the time is desirable. Thus, two bags per person - one medium to large size and a small carry bag - would serve the purpose of safety and care too. This carry bag has an advantage during actual sightseeing when the main luggage component would normally be kept in the hotel. It can also be used to carry water bottles, cameras, medicines, etc. Bags with good quality wheels are necessary as at many places we have to carry them with us. Since we were going to stay and travel in Germany the 49-Euro travel pass on our mobiles was a must. The travel pass was extensively used. As we were to travel through the DB trains it was necessary that the bags had wheels and were easy to carry. With this care and adequate euros credited to the Forex cards we were all set before the travel began.

THE PLANNING

It was during 2023 that we visited the UK and Ireland. My book covering this tour is already available. As a traveler, I usually choose 2 to 3 countries to travel, so that I can explore them in-depth, relish, enjoy them, and most importantly spend sufficient time so that I can write about my travel experience. This time we chose Germany. Considering the currency exchange rate and a one-time and one-country visit we preferred Germany and planned to visit it in May 2024. For Germany, we already had our bio-identification, which includes the eyes and fingerprints, done for the EU during our last visit in 2022 with a validity period of 5 years. As part of our usual procedure, we contacted Mr Ratnadeep Todkar from Samarth Holidays Kolhapur and had regular follow-ups with him and his assistant to see that the formalities to be complied with before applying for the visa are completed. While planning the tour, care had to be taken to ensure availability of sufficient time to explore the cities of our visit on foot. We had about four sittings to finalize and book all the hotels, and tickets and keep the money required for our tour ready. The roles played by my friend Umesh Kuber and his Daughter Shruti Kuber were vital in all our planning. The booking of tickets, Hotels and Travel plans, etc. were meticulously planned. We started to search for a suitable flight schedule and a competitive airfare and found the Lufthansa direct flight to Frankfurt to be suitable on both these requirements. Using the relevant websites we booked hotels.

THE TRAVEL PLAN

Date	Start	End	From	To	Mode of transport	Remark
10/05/2024	9.00 AM.	12.30 P.M.	Kolhapur Star Air Flight S5162	Mumbai Airport and to Fab Hotels Andheri East	Flight and Car	
	10.00 PM	10.30 PM.	Fab Hotels Andheri East	CSMIA Mumbai	Car	
11/05/2024	2.45 A.M.	8.15 A.M.	Mumbai	Frankfurt Airport	Flight LH0757	
			Frankfurt Airport	Hotel Scandic Frankfurt Museumsufer	Train	DB Monthly Ticket
12/05/2024	9.30 A.M.	12.00 Noon	Frankfurt HBF	Stuttgart HBF	Train	
	12.40 PM	1.30 PM.	Stuttgart HBF	Gastehaus Andra	Train and Bus	
13/05/2024	9.30 A.M.	12.00 Noon	Stuttgart HBF	Triberg	Train	Visit tourist places in Triberg
	4.30 PM.	6.00 PM.	Triberg HBF	Stuttgart HBF		
14/05/2024	9.00 AM.	8.00 PM	Gastehaus Andra	Gastehaus Andra	Bus and Train	Visit tourist attractions in Stuttgart
15/-5/2024	9.30 A.M.	12.30 PM.	Stuttgart HBF	Munich HBF	Bus and Train	
			Munich HBF	Hotel Das Seidl		
16/05/2024	9.00 AM.	11.30 AM.	Munich HBF	Garmisch Partenkirchen HBF	Bus and Train	Visit Tourist Attractio

	5.30 PM.	7.30 PM.	Garmisch Partenkirchen HBF	Munich HBF		ns in Garmisch Partenkirchen
17/05/2024	9.00 AM.	8.00 PM	Hotel Das Seidl	Hotel Das Seidl	Bus and Train	Visit tourist attractions in Munich
18/05/2024	9.00 AM. 2.00 PM	12.30 PM. 8.00 PM	Munich HBF IBIS Nurenburg	Nurenburg HBF IBIS Nurenburg	Bus and Train	Visit tourist attractions in Nurenburg
19/05/2024	9.00 AM. 2.00 PM	1.30 PM. 8.00 PM	Nurenburg HBF Hotel H2	Leipzig HBF Hotel H2	Bus and Train	Visit tourist attractions in Leipzig
20/05/2024	9.00 AM. 3.00 PM.	1.30 PM. 8,00 PM.	Leipzig HBF Holiday Inn Express	Berlin HBF Holiday Inn Express	Bus and Train	Visit tourist attractions in Berlin
21/05/2024	9.00 AM.	8.00 PM	Holiday Inn Express	Holiday Inn Express	Bus and Train	Visit tourist attractions in Berlin
22/05/2024	9.00 AM.	8.00 PM	Holiday Inn Express	Holiday Inn Express	Bus and Train	Visit tourist attractions in Berlin

23/06/2024	9.00 AM.	11.00 AM.	Berlin HBF	Potsdam HBF	Bus and Train	Visit tourist attractions in Potsdam
	6.00 PM.	8.00 PM	Potsdam HBF	Berlin HBF		
24/05/2024	9.00 AM.	1.30 PM.	Berlin HBF	Hamburg HBF	Bus and Train	Visit tourist attractions in Hamburg
	3.00 PM.	8.00 PM.	Hotel Wilhelm Busch	Hotel Wilhelm Busch		
25/05/2024	9.00 AM.	8.00 PM.	Hotel Wilhelm Busch	Hotel Wilhelm Busch	Bus and Train	Visit tourist attractions in Hamburg
26/05/2024	9.00 AM.	5.00 PM.	Hamburg HBF	Cologne HBF	Bus and Train	
27/05/2024	9.00 AM.	8.00 PM.	Holiday Inn Express Mulheim Cologne	Holiday Inn Express Mulheim Cologne	Bus and Train	Visit tourist attractions in Cologne
28/05/2024	9.00 AM.	11.00 AM.	Cologne HBF	Bruhl HBF	Bus and Train	Visit tourist attractions in Bruhl
	5.00 PM.	7.00 PM.	Bruhl HBF	Cologne HBF		
29/05/2024	9.00 AM.	12.30 PM.	Cologne HBF	Frankfurt HBF	Bus and Train	Visit tourist attractions in Frankfurt
	2.00 PM.	8.00 PM.	Park-inn by Radisson	Park-inn by Radisson		
30/5/2024	9.00 AM.	11.00 AM.	Frankfurt HBF	Heidelburg HBF	Bus and Train	Visit tourist attractions in

	12.10 PM..	7.00 PM.	Heidelburg HBF	Frankfurt HBF		Heidelburg
31/05/2024	9.00 AM.	8.00 PM.	Park-inn by Radisson	Park-inn by Radisson	Bus and Train	Visit tourist attractions in Frankfurt
01/06/2024	10.00 AM.	1.30 PM	Park-inn by Radisson	Frankfurt Airport	Bus and Flight	LH0756
02/06/2024		1.30 AM.	CSMIA Mumbai			
	9.00 AM.	11.00 AM.	CSMIA Mumbai	Kolhapur Airport	Flight	Star Air S5161

KOLHAPUR TO MUMBAI

10th May 2024 – Friday. We started from our home in Kolhapur to reach the airport to catch the Star Air flight S5162 to Mumbai. The flight was at 10.30 AM. and was on time. We reached Mumbai at 11.30 am. Taking a cab reached the pre-booked hotel, Fab hotel Royal International, Brahans Business Park near Mahakali Caves Road, Andheri East. Since the flight was at night we preferred to take rest and paid a small visit to the Vile Parle East area to buy a few essential things. We had our dinner in the hotel and left for the T2 terminal of the Mumbai Airport at about 10 P.M. Fortunately, the check-in, security and emigration part was easy and not as time-consuming as it used to be. The facilities for the priority pass holders at the airport Lounge have now become a big problem. We were not happy with the procedure because of which not only could we not get entry but also many of the travellers did not get entry. It may be because of limited space at the lounge and some technical issue with the cards. We went to the gate that we were supposed to reach and had some rest there before boarding the flight. The flight was early morning next day i.e. on 11th May 2024.

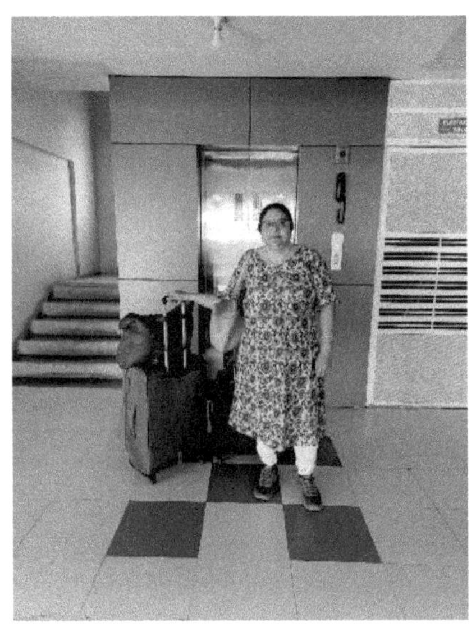

At our Kolhapur Home

At Vile Parle Mumbai

Since we were in Andheri we thought of visiting Vile Parle, an area very close to Andheri. We were familiar with it coincidentally. We took an auto to reach Vile Parle East station area and bought a few things that were necessary for our tour.

FRANKFURT - RUDESHEIM

11th May –Saturday. The Lufthansa flight LH 757 was at 2.45 AM and accordingly our boarding process began on time. The flight left in time and we were served dinner which is a standard amenity for most international flights. Post dinner we took some rest before we reached Frankfurt at 8.15 am. We had already booked our hotel in Frankfurt and after clearing all the necessary formalities at the airport, in particular the immigration and the bag collection, we planned to go to the city centre by S8 or S9 train from the airport train station.

Kolhapur Airport

CSMIA Mumbai

Frankfurt HBF

At Punnet Iyer's House in Frankfurt

The hotel was very close to the main train station but before we went to the hotel we purchased two SIM cards for our mobiles so that we remain connected with the trains, hotels and Google Maps to visit the sites. After purchasing the cards and activating them we reached the hotel. The usual check-in is after about 2 PM and we were there quite before time. We could keep the bags there but the room were to be allotted in the afternoon. Fortunately, Sharddha's friend's daughter lived in Frankfurt and we were supposed to give her sweets and clothes. We had established contact with her well in advance and had a detailed discussion about the route and tram to take and the stop to get down. She advised us to take tram 16 from the HBF area and get down at the last stop. We followed her advice. This was our second train experience after we used the S8/S9 to reach the main train station. Shraddha's friend's daughter Mrs Amita Iyer came to receive us at the last stop from where we walked to her house. She lives with her husband Puneet Iyer and their son Riyan. A small beautiful family. They prepared lunch which was beautiful and Indian style - Rice, Dal, and a special south Indian subji. After lunch was over and as we were just chatting, Puneet enquired about our day's programme. As we had not planned any programme for that day we told him that nothing was planned. He then asked us about our readiness for a half-day tour. Even though we had travelled the full previous night, we indicated our readiness, and accordingly, we planned a half-day trip on our first day at Frankfurt. We went together since they had a holiday for a trip to Rudesheim on the river Rhein's bank. None of us had to book any tickets so we started from home and reached the Main station to catch the train to the destination. Our train travelled initially along the coast of River Main and then the Rhine. Rüdesheim am Rhein is a German winemaking town in the Rhine Gorge and part of the UNESCO World Heritage Site in this region. It lies in the Rheingau-Taunus-Kreis district in the Regierungsbezirk of Darmstadt, Hessen. Known as Rüdesheim, it is officially Rüdesheim am Rhein, to distinguish it from Rüdesheim an der Nahe. It is a major tourist attraction, especially for foreign visitors. Rüdesheim lies at the foot of the Niederwald on the Rhine's right bank in the Rheingau wine region. The town belongs to the Frankfurt Rhine Main Region and to the World Heritage Site Rhine Gorge. It has a picturesque Old Town, located in the Rheingau landscape celebrated in Rhine romanticism. In 1877, the first foundation stone was laid for the Niederwalddenkmal, a patriotic monument above the vineyards which would be finished in 1883. It attracted many tourists who could reach it on a cog railway. Today, a gondola lift brings visitors up to the monument. Tourism has increasingly replaced shipping as a source of income. A well-known tradition is the Weinkönigin ("Wine Queen") with her princesses. Each year in the summertime, the Rüdesheim wine festival is held, whose highlights include the Wine Queen's and the princesses' coronation. They represent the town of Rüdesheim and its wine in other communities and winegrowing areas.

A sculpture at the city center

The cable ride on the mountain

On the Rhine Cruise

With the entire group.

It takes about 1.5 hrs to reach the stop. After we got down we walked to the city centre, where there was a church and local eateries. Puneet had booked a cruise on the Rhine river which was of about 40 to 45 min. The cruise terminal was close to where we had reached and then we took the cruise watching the forts and the grape fields along the cruise. We reached a place to get down the cruise move around the small town and go back to where we had started. But at the destination we saw a cable car and thought to explore it. We booked the tickets and went up to the top of the hill.

The Castle along the River bank

The Niederwald Monument

The cable car tickets were combined with the tickets to go to the town from the Niederwald monument. The climb was high but the gondola-type sitting arrangement was no doubt enjoyable but it was open requiring proper care of and attention to children. Even light-hearted persons will not find it easy to manage the small fear that may develop. After reaching the end of the cable car ride we had to walk about 3 Km. to reach the spot of the Niederwald monument. The walk was in the forest and we could see a few animals like deer and sheep and also a lot of birds on the way. It is a big monument and there is a good valley view from that point. After a visit to the monument we were to go to the town using another set of cable cars but since it was 6 P.M. the cable cars had stopped.

The Rhine Valley   The small cities along the Rhine Valley

We missed the last one. We were on top of the hill so we had to take a walk along the slope to the city. The walk was along the grape gardens and small outhouses but the route was not a tar road, it was a walking trail with no Vehicles. It was almost 8 PM by the time we reached the town. It was clear daylight up to that time. We had our dinner at a hotel in the city centre and took the train back to Frankfurt. We reached Frankfurt around 11 PM. and walked to the hotel. After check-in we had rest. The first day was enjoyable and also exhaustive.

STUTTGART

12th May- Sunday, We started from Frankfurt main railway station (Hauptbahnhof) or HBF (for the railway station it will be mentioned as HBF in the text hereafter) in the morning after having a heavy breakfast at the hotel. We travelled in the RE55 which is a regional express (RE) towards Wurzburg and changed to RB8 to travel to Stuttgart. We had to change the train once and the connection time was also to be considered. We reached Stuttgart at about 1.00 PM. From the HBF we walked to the Hauptbahnhof Arnulf - Klett-platz, which caters to the suburban metro network. We used the U7 towards Nellinggen and after 7 stops got down at Ruhbank from where we took the bus no 70 and reached Birkheckenstr where the hotel was situated. The hotel Gastehaus Andrea is very close to the bus stop. We had done the booking well in advance and hence we could get the room keep the luggage and after getting fresh we left for the city centre. There are many places to see in the city centre and since it was Sunday the shops, hotels etc. were mostly closed but there was a Sunday fair in which there were many stalls which we could see and move around. The city centre is too big hence we could just walk around and see the main places.

Fountain and Old buildings at Stuttgart city centre

The city centre was almost destroyed during World War II. The rebuilt city has a mix of modern and historic architecture. Historic buildings include the old castle, housing the Landesmuseum, the new palace, the Rosenstein Palace, now the natural history museum, the

Gothic Leonhardskirche, of the hall type; and the Stiftskirche (collegiate church), a 12th-century Romanesque basilica completed in the Gothic style (1436–95). Outside the city centre are Solitude Palace to the west and Hohenheim Palace to the south, now occupied by the University of Hohenheim.

Monuments and buildings in Stuttgart city centre

The new castle Stuttgart

Kunstgebaude Stuttgart

At the centre of Stuttgart lies its main square, Schlossplatz. The largest square in Stuttgart, it stands at the crossover point between the city's shopping area, Schlossgarten Park which runs down to the river Neckar, Stuttgart's two central castles, and major museums and residential areas to the southwest. Königstraße, Stuttgart's most important shopping street which runs along the northwestern edge of Schlossplatz claims to be the longest pedestrianized street in Germany. The Stiftskirche (Collegiate Church), dates back to the 12th century but was changed to the Late Gothic style in the 15th century and has been a Protestant church since 1534. The exterior is Romanesque/Gothic. Altes Schloss (the Old Castle), mostly dates from the late 15th century, some parts date back to 1320 and are in the Renaissance style and are reconstructed. Alte Kanzlei (the Old Chancellery) on Schillerplatz square which backs onto the 1598 Mercury Pillar. (?) Neues Schloss (the New Castle), was completed in 1807 (Baroque/Classicism), reconstructed with a modern interior, and currently houses government offices. The cellars with a collection of stone fragments from Roman times are open to visitors. Wilhelmpalais (the King Wilhelm Palace), 1840, Königsbau (the King's Building), 1850, has been housing the "Königsbau Passagen" shopping centre since 2006, The Großes Haus of Stuttgart National Theatre, Markthalle Market Hall, 1910. The Hauptbahnhof (Main Railway Station) was designed in 1920, its stark, functional lines are typical of the artistic trend 'Neue Sachlichkeit' (New Objectivity). The Württembergische Landesbibliothek state library, was rebuilt in 1970. Friedrichsbau Varieté (Friedrich Building), was rebuilt in 1994 on the site of the former Art Nouveau building reconstructed with a simplified interior after World War II. Examples of modern architecture include the Weissenhof Estate (1927), the town hall, the 633-foot (193-meter) television tower (1955), and the Stuttgarter Liederhall concert and congress hall, built during 1954–56. It is in the area around the new castle that the Sunday market or the weekly fair is held. We arrived in the evening and the fair was open to some extent but was to close shortly. There were many local items, food, and other things for sale. Since we were there in the city centre, we could see the places in that area. The daylight was almost up to 9 PM. Places like Scholssplatz, Old Castle, Karsplatz, Carls Braughous, Kunstgebaude Stuttgart, the Staatstheater, Aussicht, Schauspiel, and the Konigstrase are in that region and we could see them from outside. We could see the sculptures, gardens, and buildings while walking around the New Palace area. The Kings Strasse or Kings Street is the main shopping street very close to the castle area. The street has a double line of trees with fountains, places to sit, hotels, cafes, bars, and fashion shops. This is a good street to walk around. We searched for a food stall but only the McDonald's was open and hence we had to take some food from there and then either carry it to our room or eat it there. We chose to have it there itself as the time required to travel to the hotel would take about an hour. We walked from Kings Street to the HBF, the S Bahn station, and took the required metro to reach the place to change over to the bus and reached the hotel. By the time we reached the Hotel, it was 9.30 PM. No doubt it was daylight but considering the next day's travel take a rest. We were given the back door keys of the hotel so that we could enter inside at any time.

Statue at Stuttgart City centre

Fountain on the Kingsstrass Stuttgart

TRIBERG

13th May, Monday. As planned for the day we were to visit the Place called Triberg which is about 2.5 hours away from Stuttgart. We reached the Stuttgart HBF and then the train RE1 to Karlsruhe HBF from where the RE2 was taken to reach Triberg. The journey was through the black forest region. It was all green with thick woods and plenty of water sources along the track. From Triberg HBF we took the bus with No 550 to the Hinterbrag. The 5th stop is Wallfahrtsstrase and the falls is very close to the stop, almost 450 meters by walk. Triberg is a small town in the Black Forest, Germany, located in the Schwarzwald-Baar district. If you were to look at a map, it's around the middle of the forest, sitting between 500 and 1038 meters above sea level.

The House of 1000 Clocks

At the Triberg fantasy

Thanks to its central location, it's fairly easily visited not only from West Germany, but also from Switzerland and the Alsace region of France. Billed as the highest waterfall in Germany, this is a popular place for most visitors to Triberg, and for good reason. While it's not technically the highest (that honour goes to the Röthbachfall), at 162 meters it's certainly one of the tallest accessible waterfalls, with water cascading down 7 steps into the valley below. Despite being a paid attraction, the waterfall has retained much of its natural beauty and is an ideal place to while away some time. The main entrance to the waterfall is easily reached on foot from the main high street and is also clearly signposted. There are three clearly marked trails covering the park where the waterfalls are, all of varying lengths and difficulties, the longest being around 2 hours. However, reaching the waterfalls themselves is incredibly easy. There is a ticket for the entrance to the waterfalls at the gate itself. This ticket also includes entrance to a few more attractions in the city. Once you enter you go up the path on a small hill and you will be at the bottom of the falls in a few minutes. As the waterfall does not come straight down, you will need to walk higher to see the top, but the path is well-maintained and has a low difficulty level (even for children).

Near the Triberg Museum

The famous Triberg waterfall

At the entrance, you can also buy bags of peanuts that you can feed to the waterfall's friendly resident squirrels. We could see a few of them on our way. We reached the main viewing point for the falls. A few tourists were taking photographs, which we also did. For Bird-lovers, like us, we could see the numerous nutcrackers that roost in the surrounding trees, and also a few more species. Then we chose the path crossing the water and we entered the zoo area. Just close to the zoo, there was a craftsman's cabin or shop, he was preparing the cuckoo clocks and other things. We could discuss with him, how it is prepared, how much time it takes, what is the cost and how much the demand is for the clocks, etc. Just close to it is the black forest museum. Then we went to the Schwarzwald Museum (black forest museum) which was on the way. The admission to this museum is included with your admission to the waterfalls. Described as an interactive model attraction, visitors are invited to trigger and watch the models of vehicles, trains, and cable cars covering its 300 sqm space. Included amongst the models is a replica of Triberg railway station and a miniature 'Wasserfall Express' train. There are also models of various other sites in the Black Forest along with other regions, including a beach scene of Lake Constance. Another one of Triberg's most well-known attractions, you can't miss this eccentric cuckoo clock shop with a giant cuckoo clock and moving, oversized bears adorning its exterior. While, in essence, it's a glorified souvenir shop, the House of 1000 Clocks is still worth a visit. No matter what your thoughts on the famous cuckoo clock, you can't help but be impressed by the craftsmanship as you walk along its jam-packed walls. There are also little faux 'workshop' areas where you can see videos of the wood carvers in action and look at carved wood in the earlier stages of production. Then we went to the Triberg Fantasy which is very close to the museum.

The Cuckoo Clock

The Triberg waterfall

There are many displays in which we can get ourselves for photographs. It is basically a photographic fantasy but interesting. There is a big cake, cow, flowers, horse carriage, umbrella, beer racks and many more things. We had a few photographs there. The house of 1000 clocks is just opposite this place where we could go and see the displays. Then there is a black forest speciality that is the black forest cake which is worth an experience. We had to go to a coffee shop and find out whether it was available or not and then taste it. The cake contains a layer of local wine mixed in it. It tastes beautiful. As we were tasting the cake it started raining and so using the rain kit that we had carried we reached the bus stop and waited for the bus to come and take us to the Triberg HBF. We asked the persons at the tourist office about the biggest cuckoo clock, it was far away from the HBF and had limited connectivity. We dropped the idea of seeing the biggest clock and following the route that we had taken with a little change and reached Stuttgart HBF. We reached at about 7 PM. and had some time at disposal to visit the city centre. We had seen a few places on the previous day and therefore we could see some more attractions which were a distance away from the city centre. What we did was to visit a few more places in the Stuttgart city centre. The expansive Schlossplatz is the focal point of the city. Flanking the Old Palace is Schillerplatz, an old town square with a monument to Friedrich Schiller, poet, philosopher, historian, and dramatist - one of Germany's most famous cultural giants. The bold design of the Kunstmuseum Stuttgart's large glass cube stands in sharp contrast to the palaces and other buildings overlooking the Schlossplatz. Originally laid out in 1939 as part of a major horticultural show. The Stiftkirche, Markthalle, Karlsplatz, History Museum, and Childrens Museum which are in the Old Castle, Stuttgart University, and shopping centres along the path. We had a good Dinner at the city centre and return to our hotel.

STUTTGART

14th May Tuesday. We saw the city center but then there are many more things to see around Stuttgart for which the tourist Museum pass is the best option. One does not have to stand in the queue and it also becomes more economical than individual tickets. We thought of buying the Stuttgart museum pass for one day, accordingly, we left the hotel and reached the city centre at 10 AM when the office opened and collected the day pass which cost us 24 euros per person. We first planned to visit the palace which was outside the city. North of Stuttgart, in the small city of Ludwigsburg, is the vast and lavishly decorated Ludwigsburg Palace, one of Germany's largest and loveliest Baroque palaces. Ludwigsburg Residential Palace (Residenzschloss Ludwigsburg) is one of the few Baroque buildings to have survived the tumultuous history of the last centuries almost unscathed. This truly palatial complex stands out not just for its impressive size, but also for its sumptuous interiors. Another feature is the unique blend of three different architectural styles: Baroque, Rococo, and Neoclassicism. A wide variety of museums and exhibitions, for both young and old, help to make Ludwigsburg Residential Palace a popular tourist attraction, the Keramikmuseum (Ceramics Museum) houses a large collection, the Modemuseum (Fashion Museum) showcases clothing from the 18th century to the 20th, the private apartments of Duke Carl Eugen, with their original décor, boast rare and valuable furniture and accessories; and the Barockgalerie (Baroque Gallery) features an array of historical works by a selection of artists. Kinderreich is an interactive museum where young visitors are positively encouraged to touch the exhibits and try things for themselves. Children aged four years and up can dress up and learn about life in the Duke's court. The first palace on the site, which forms the old corps de logis, or main part of the building, was constructed from 1704 onwards. It was intended as a hunting lodge for Duke Eberhard Ludwig. In 1718, however, when Ludwigsburg became the Duke's principal place of residence, he sought a more fitting reflection of his power and prestige. Donato Giuseppe Frisoni, who was responsible for the construction of the palace, also developed plans for a new corps de logis to the south. As a result, the three-wing complex acquired a fourth wing, enclosing a square. The impressive structure was completed in 1733. A walk through the palace's grand rooms is time traveling in style, the magnificent interiors offer a glimpse of life in the Baroque, Rococo, and Neoclassical eras. In these authentic period surroundings, imbued with a subtle sense of faded glory, you can relive the days when Ludwigsburg was a regal residence and the centre of the duchy of Württemberg. The Schlosstheater (palace theatre) in the eastern wing is a particular highlight of the palace. With almost intact stage machinery and stage decoration, it is one of Europe's oldest theatres. The four additional museums, which were opened on the palace's 300th anniversary in 2004, are further attractions. The Baroque also comes to life in the large park that surrounds the palace on three sides. The gardens were reconstructed in 1954 in honor of the palace's 250th birthday, partly in their historic design, partly following Baroque ideas. Since then, the "Blooming Baroque" and its fairy tale garden have been a popular destination. The park surrounding the charming pleasure palace, Ludwigsburg Favourite Palace, invites visitors to take a stroll.

The Ludwigsburg Palace

The Ludwigsburg Palace

From there, a romantic three-kilometre avenue leads to the Monrepos Lakeside Palace. We used the S Bahn to reach Ludwigsburg which takes about half an hour to reach. After reaching the Ludwigberg HBF we used the local transport to reach the palace area. We saw a beautiful garden but a separate ticket was required for entry to the garden. We chose to visit the palace only and were allowed entry but found that the inner part of the palace can be seen only in a guided tour. There are guided tours every hour alternatively in English and German. Since our slot was in the German language we used the headphones for translation. This is possibly the only palace that has not been damaged during the WWII bombing. The procedure for visiting the palace is interesting. The group with the guide walks to the main gate on one side and then the locked door is opened for the tourists and as the tourists enter inside the door is locked. Then only one side of the palace was open to visitors. There are large rooms, decorations, wooden furniture, clothes, a big hall, churches and many more things inside as mentioned earlier. We were on the tour only for one of the wings in the palace. It is almost one hour walking tour after which we come out through the door on the other side. We had started from Stuttgart HBF at about 10.30 AM and now it was almost 12 noon. We took the train to return to Stuttgart HBF and the next item on our itinerary was the Mercedes Benz museum. By taking a suitable metro and crossing the river Neckar we reached the museum. It is an ultra-modern museum. The current building, which stands directly outside the main gate of the Daimler factory in Stuttgart, was designed by UN Studio. It is based on a unique cloverleaf concept using three overlapping circles with the centre removed to form a triangular atrium recalling the shape of a Wankel engine. The building was completed and opened on 19 May 2006. Architecture and exhibition concepts are closely interwoven, as exhibition designer HG Merz had already been commissioned before the architecture competition in 2001. The building's height and "double helix" interior were designed to maximize space, providing 16,500 square meters (178,000 sq ft) of exhibition space on a footprint of just 4,800 square metres (52,000 sq ft). The double helix also corresponds to the exhibition concept, which divides the museum into the "legend rooms" and the "collections", offering two alternative tours that can be merged at any given point in the museum. The museum contains more than 160 vehicles, some dating back to the very earliest days of the motorcar engine. The vehicles are maintained by the Mercedes-Benz Classic Centre of Fellbach. Previously, the museum was housed in a dedicated building within the factory complex and visitors had in recent decades been transported from the main gate by a secured shuttle. Since the ticket was included in the Day pass, we entered the museum and we could see the progress in the automobile industry during the last 200-odd years. There were small carts, big buses, the latest model cars to racing cars with all types of accessories. The walls, when we walk inside the museum, depict the history of various treaties and advancements that took place during WWI and WWII and the industrial revolutions etc. marking the history of the region. The Mercedes-Benz Museum celebrates that more than 130 years of automotive history in over 1500 exhibits that cover nine floors and put the invention and development of the automobile into the context of each era's technology, daily life, and society. It takes quite some time to see the museum. After the museum, we were on the way to the famous Wilhelma garden in Stuttgart with a variety of plants and animals. But as we were crossing the river we could see the am. Leuze Mineralbad and we knew that the pass included a free experience of this place for 2 hrs. We exactly did not know what this was, but we contacted the reception desk and came to know that the complex has thermal hot spring water which is in the swimming pools, and the temperatures are kept different depending upon the pool. DAS LEUZE in Stuttgart guarantees first-class bathing enjoyment, with a total of eight swimming and bathing pools and over 1700 square metres of water area in the in- and outdoor mineral pools.

The Mercedes Benz Museum

Inside the Mercedes Benz museum

And thanks to the therapeutic properties of the mineral water, a visit here also promotes good health. Wellness, warmth, and well-being await you, dry, aroma and outdoor saunas, steam rooms, adventure showers, and lots more besides providing relaxation and help you recover from the daily grind. A sauna with a view, the "Winzersauna" is sure to delight with a variety of sauna rooms and a panoramic view of the Neckar and the surrounding vineyards. At the LEUZE Mineralbad in Stuttgart, two highly carbonated healing springs and a mineral spring are used for swimming and saunas. The temperatures range from 31^0C to 27^0C and there are 7 to 9 pools with varying temperatures and also an open area, there is also a sauna area but we did not have the pass to enter the area. We enjoyed the pools and the thermal treatment for 2 hours. Fortunately, we were carrying the swimming suit with us which we could use. This visit to the Lauzebad relaxed us. From there we came to the Wilhema garden, which was included in the pass and we could get entry into the garden. A unique combination of zoo and botany awaits you in Germany's only zoological and botanical garden - Wilhelma Stuttgart. Here you can observe around 11,000 animals of around 1,200 species. This makes Wilhelma one of the most species-rich zoos not only in Germany but also worldwide. However, it is not only the many animals that make Wilhelma exceptional but also the plants. Approximately 8,500 plant species and varieties showcase the lush diversity of nature. Everything is framed by the historic park, which invites you to dream with its Moorish-style buildings. The garden and the buildings with the flair of 1001 Nights were laid out in 1842 under King Wilhelm I of Württemberg. After a large part of the complex was destroyed in the Second World War, Wilhelma gradually transformed from a botanical garden into a zoological-botanical garden but still allows you to feel the splendor of times gone by. You will find worthwhile attractions and reasons to visit Wilhelma at any time of year: In March, the largest magnolia grove north of the Alps blooms here. In spring and summer, you can observe many small animals. In the colder months of the year, the warm greenhouses and animal houses are an attraction. But there are also impressive sights for botanists:

The Lauze bad

Inside the Wilhema Garden

The water lilies in the 650 square meter pond in the Moorish Garden are the largest in the world and can bear a weight of up to 70 kilograms on a single leaf. And you can marvel at giant sequoia trees that were planted in the middle of the 19th century. Today one of Germany's largest zoos, with more than two million annual visitors, Wilhelma Zoological and Botanic Garden was created as a private royal retreat for the Swabian King Wilhelm I. It is a very big garden and a variety of plants, there are greenhouses, a zoo, an aquarium, and many more places. It was evening by the time we came out from the garden.

Inside the Wilhema Garden   Sclpture inside the Ludwigberg Palace

Then the last place to visit was the TV tower which was on the way to our hotel. Taking the buses and trains we reached the TV tower which was included in the pass. We could go to the top of the tower which is at a height of 217 meters but the time taken to reach there was only a few seconds. It is very fast. There are binoculars, hotel and platforms to see the city from the top. We could see the entire city in 360 degrees and due to the height and the distance from the spot, it was beautiful to watch. After the TV tower we used the bus service to reach our hotel. We had dinner in the hotel itself. This was our last day in Stuttgart. We were scheduled to go to Munich for the next halt.

MUNICH

15th May, Wednesday. We started from Stuttgart HBF in the morning and taking RE5 towards Friedrichshafen Stadt reached Ulm HBF where we had to change over to RE9 for Munich. After studying the route we came to know that we could get down one stop earlier and then take a bus to reach our hotel instead of going to Munich and coming back. We got down at Pasing which is a stop before the Munich HBF. From passing we reached Lochhausen by S Bahn and then by taking bus 830 reached Northerndtrad. The hotel Das Seidl - Hotel and Tagung is very close to the stop. We reached the hotel around 1 PM. After check-in, we had tea, took the bus 830 and got down at the S Bahn stop to reach the city centre to visit Martin Platz. As we came out of the stop we could see the main square of the city. The Martin Platz was just in front of us. It is one of the main buildings in the city and at the centre of the city. There is a lot of space in front of the Platz because at 11 AM, 12 Noon, and 5 PM there is a puppet show on the tower of the Martin Platz. Since there was heavy rush we were unable to see it properly so it was planned to witness the event the next day and also record it. From there we walked to the Fraunkirche which is very close to it. The Munich city pass costs 24.90 euros. Marienplatz has been Munich's central square since the city's foundation, the site of medieval jousting tournaments, and until 1807, where markets were held. Munich's English Garden is not only the largest city park in Germany - it covers an area of 910 acres - it's also one of the most beautiful. Then we walked towards the St Peter church, toy museum, and Viktualiemarkt, the famous open market for food and beer. Then we took a small walk in the English garden and then towards the Max Joseph Platz and then the city centre. This was a big walk and we were to see the stadiums on the last day with the pass. We searched for a suitable hotel to have food and returned to the hotel, as the next day was going to be very busy. We were to go to the place called Garmisch-Partenkirchen. A write-up on Garmisch-Partenkirchen is given in the write-up and then the write-up about the city of Munich will continue.

GARMISCH PARTENKIRCHEN

16th May, Thursday. We started from the hotel and reached Munich HBF to catch the train RB6 to Garmisch-Partenkirchen. RB6 takes less than 2 hours to reach the destination. We were there at the destination at about 11.30 AM. The Zugspitze is the highest peak in Germany. Unfortunately, the cogwheel train which starts from Garmisch-Partenkirchen was closed for that week due to maintenance work but we reached Eibsee which is at the base of the peak. There is a cable car to reach the peak but due to the maintenance work of the rail, even this cable car was closed for maintenance.

The cable car to the Zugspitze

Peak The Zugspitze Peak

The Zugspitze peak

The Eibsee Lake

The Zugspitze peak   The Zugspitze peak

We were not lucky enough to be able to go to the peak and had to be satisfied just by viewing it from Eibsee. Zugspitze, a mountain on the border between Germany and Austria, is the highest point (9,718 feet [2,962 meters]) in Germany. Zugspitze is part of the Wettersteingebirge in the Bavarian Alps. The mountain is approached on the west by an aerial tramway (built 1924–26) from the village of Eibsee, and on the northeast by a railway from the town of Garmisch-Partenkirchen, both in Germany. The peak is noted for its scenic beauty and for its winter (skiing) and summer (climbing) activities. There is a meteorological observatory on the mountain. The mountains hold lignite mines and petroleum deposits and are crossed at Scharnitz Pass (3,133 feet [955 metres]) by road and railway and at Achen Pass (3,087 feet [941 metres]) by road. Tourism and winter sports are the region's main activities. A large national park preserves the original Alpine landscape, plants, and animals from the steady encroachment of urbanization. The "Zugspitze Round Trip" is a unique opportunity for visitors of all ages to visit Germany's highest mountain using the cable cars of Bayerische Zugspitzbahn Bergbahn AG. The ride on the Cable car Zugspitze, the cogwheel train and the Gletscherbahn cable car includes breath-taking views of the surrounding mountains and valleys. The restaurants at the summit and on the Zugspitze plateau offer refreshments. At the Photo-stop Zugspitze, you can also capture your visit to the summit on camera. Almost immediately upon its opening, it became one of the most popular places to visit from Garmisch-Partenkirchen. Even though we could not visit the peak, the houses along the road were beautiful, there were many different things we could see during our road journey which reflected the culture and traditions of the region.

Houses along the route to Eibsee

This region also has a good connection with the black forest traditions. The Peak has a border with Austria and the cable car from that end might be working but from the German side, both the cogwheel train and the cable car were under repair. An excellent way to get the most out of your sightseeing and hiking high above Garmisch-Partenkirchen is to make use of the town's fantastic network of summit lifts and gondolas. But the maintenance work did not allow us to enjoy the peaks and other places. Another famous resident, Richard Strauss, spent 40 years of his life in Garmisch-Partenkirchen. Today, his lovely 1908 Art Nouveau villa in Garmisch is a museum and memorial dedicated to the great conductor and composer who lived and died here. This fascinating little museum on Ludwigstrasse was started in 1895 and is housed in a 17th-century former merchant's home. After enjoying the Eibsee Lake we found some beautiful tracking, cycling, and other adventure sports facilities but they were not suitable for our fitness level. We walked around the lake and then took the bus to return to Garmisch-Partenkirchen and after going around in the city took the train to Munich. We reached Munich at around 4 PM. We chose to visit the tourist information center and take the museum pass for the next day so that we could start our visits to the palaces as early as possible. Next day we took a metro to reach the city centre where we had been on the previous day but had missed the puppet show. We reached the Marineplatz and enjoyed and also recorded the puppet show on the tower. Glockenspiel is the show that starts in the New Rathaus which is the Marineplatz.

Inside the Frauenkirche Munich   Viktualienmarkt

The Glockenspiel in the New Town Hall tower shows two events from Munich's city history. First, the wedding of Duke Wilhelm V and Renate of Lorraine, and celebrated in February 1568. In honor of the bride and groom, a jousting tournament took place on Marienplatz. The Bavarian knight triumphed over his opponent from Lorraine. The lower floor shows the Schäffler dance. After a severe plague epidemic, the barrel makers are said to have been the first to venture out into the streets again, dancing to amuse the plague-stricken population. After observing the event at the New Rathous we started walking around the area and visited a few more places in the region. We went to Viktualienmarkt, the beer and October Fest museum, the national theatre, the opera house, Alter Hof, Hofbrauhaus, Odeonsplatz, Hofgarden, and a few more places before it became too late to reach the hotel and take rest. The next day since we had the museum pass we started with the baroque palace of Nymphenburg. This is on north east side of Munich. It is a very big palace and has a beautiful garden. Nymphenburg Palace owes its foundation as a summer residence to the birth of the long-awaited heir to the throne, Max Emanuel, who was born in 1662 to the Bavarian Elector Ferdinand Maria and his wife, Henriette Adelaide of Savoy, after some ten years of marriage. Nymphenburg Palace acquired its present-day dimensions under the elector Max Emanuel. Supervised by the court architect Henrico Zuccalli, two offset pavilions were built on each side of the existing structure, to the north and south. Begun in 1701, the pavilions were linked with the central edifice by galleries. Of the measures that were implemented then, the following are the most notable, the central pavilion as the focal point of the ensemble was redesigned, the royal apartments were furnished and decorated, the annexes, situated in front of the main palace, were rebuilt as residences for court officials and the crescent was constructed with a circular wall and five pairs of pavilions. Radiating out from the centre, the perspectively off-set structures fused to form a completely symmetrical "ideal town" that could accommodate the royal household.

Frauenkirche Munich

The Marianplatz

After 1715, and following the plans of Dominique Girard and Joseph Effner, the park was also redesigned and extended, giving it its present dimensions and Baroque style. Karl Albrecht, first as Elector of Bavaria and then as Emperor Charles VII, continued the construction work at Nymphenburg begun by his father. He enhanced the complex by adding the palace's crescent. Both the palace and crescent were intended to form the centre of a planned "Carlstadt" ("Charles Town"). Under Elector Maximilian III Joseph, the Great Hall at Nymphenburg Palace acquired the opulent decoration that can be admired today. Here Johann Baptist Zimmermann, together with François Cuvilliés the Elder, created a major work of Munich court Rococo. The vaulted ceiling of the Palace Chapel was also painted. Finally, under Max III Joseph, the Nymphenburg Porcelain Manufactory moved into its present quarters at the front of the palace. At this time the park, too, was given a new look. The Grand Parterre was remodeled and adorned with statues of the most important gods of Olympus. The exterior flights of steps, also date from this period and form a suitably representative entrance to the main building and Great Hall. Since it was slightly rainy we chose to see the main museum and the museum on the left side of the palace. Both contained antique collections with beautifully decorated large halls used by the kings for different types of meetings, banquets, music, dance, etc. There were horse carriages and precious ornaments and porcelain which they called white gold. After visiting this palace we started our journey to the next place to visit and it was the famous Deutsches museum. Deutsches Museum, a museum of science and industry established in Munich in 1903 and opened on Museumsinsel (Museum Island) in 1925. Its pattern of organization and administration became the model for such later institutions as the Museum of Science and Industry in Chicago.

Bavarian state Chancellery   Bavarian State Opera House

The Deutsches Museum owes its existence to the perseverance and initiative of Oskar von Miller, who convinced industry and government authorities of the usefulness of his idea and built up the museum over two decades. Many of its valuable collections in the history of technology and the physical sciences were destroyed during World War II, but they were later replaced. The early 1980s saw severe damage to several exhibits due to arson resulting in the smallest exhibit space of 34,140 square meters (8½ acres). This was followed by an extensive reconstruction effort and additional building bringing the total exhibit space to 55,000 square meters by 1993.

The Nymphenburg Palace front view   Inside the Nymphenburg Palace

The 1980s and '90s also brought agreements with the Science Centre in Bonn and the government resulting in the creation of Deutsches Museum Bonn and the Flugwerft Schleißheim airfield exhibit. In 1996, the Bavarian Government gave buildings at the historic Theresienhöhe site in Munich to the Deutsches Museum resulting in the creation of the new transportation museum, the Deutsches Museum Verkehrszentrum, which opened in 2003 and now houses the road vehicle and train exhibits that were removed from the original Deutsches Museum site. The Theresienhöhe Quarter is a new area on the edge of the inner city of Munich, and the Museum of Transport is a part of the quarter's design of mixed-use. The Deutsches Museum began expanding in the 1990s, opening branches at Flugwerft Schleissheim (1992; "Schleissheim Airfield"), Oberschleissheim, Germany; in Bonn (1995); at Verkehrszentrum (2003; "Traffic Centre"), Munich; and in Nürnberg (2021; also called the "Future Museum"). The Deutsches Museum on Museumsinsel also houses a library, archive, publishing house, and the Kerschensteiner Kolleg, a research institute.

The Nymphenburg Palace Garden view   Inside the Nymphenburg Palace

This museum has a lot of interactive scientific collections and models. It is worth a visit specifically for the students who intend to get interactive information about the technologies. It has space, health, energy, agriculture, medicine, etc. There are almost 53 subject areas covered in the museum. The students enjoy the learning experience.

Inside the Deutsches Museum

It was almost 3 PM in the Deutsches Museum and the time to see the next museum was getting closer. We reached the Residenz museum which is a worth visit. The Residenz in central Munich is the former royal palace of the Wittelsbach monarchs of Bavaria. The Residenz is the largest city palace in Germany and is today open to visitors for its architecture, room decorations, and displays from the former royal collections. The complex of buildings contains ten courtyards and displays 130 rooms.

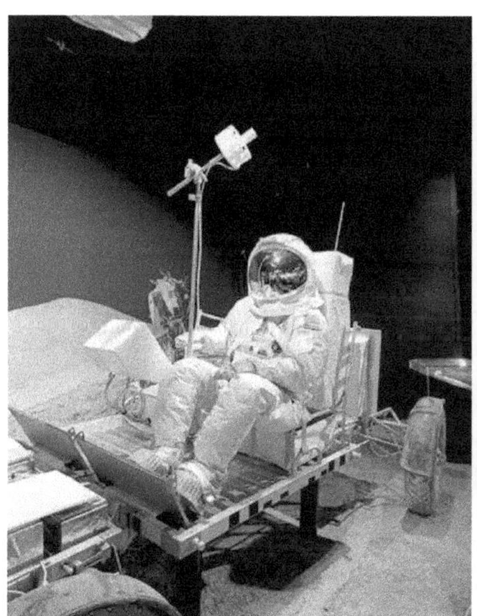

Inside the Deutsches Museum

The three main parts are the Königsbau (near the Max-Joseph-Platz), the Alte Residenz (Old Residenz; towards the Residenzstraße) and the Festsaalbau (towards the Hofgarten). A wing of the Festsaalbau contains the Cuvilliés Theatre since the reconstruction of the Residenz after World War II. It also houses the Herkulessaal (Hercules Hall), the primary concert venue for the Bavarian Radio Symphony Orchestra. The Byzantine Court Church of All Saints (Allerheiligen-Hofkirche) at the east side faces the Marstall, the building for the former Court Riding School, and the royal stables. The gothic foundation walls and the basement vaults of the old castle including the round pillars of the so-called ballroom cellar (Ballsaalkeller) are today the oldest surviving parts of the palace. The Residenz's development over the centuries didn't only take place out of its main centre, the Neuveste, but in addition grew out of several single parts and extensions, the first of which used to be the Antiquarium. Finally, after more than four centuries of development, the giant palace had practically replaced a whole former city quarter with barracks, a monastery, houses, and gardens.

Inside the Residenz museum

At the Martinplatz.

It assembles the styles of the late Renaissance, as well as of Baroque, Rococo , and Neo-Classicism. Ten courtyards can be found inside the large complex, The Grotto Courtyard (Grottenhof) with the Perseus Fountain was built between 1581 and 1586 under William V (1579–1597) by Friedrich Sustris as the leading architect, and takes its name from the Grotto on the western façade of the Antiquarium. The octagonal Brunnenhof (Fountain Courtyard) served as a place for tournaments before the large Wittelsbach Fountain was erected in the middle of the courtyard in 1610. The buildings around the Kaiserhof (Emperor's Courtyard) with the Residenz Tower as a clock tower, were erected from 1612 to 1618, in the reign of Maximilian I. Both courtyards are decorated with optical illusions on the facade, the same as the facade of the Alte Residenz. The Königsbauhof (King's Building Courtyard) replaced a garden. At its eastern side, the rococo facade of the Grüne Galerie (Green Gallery) is situated, designed by François Cuvilliés the Elder in 1731–33. Other courtyards are the Kapellenhof (Chapel Courtyard), the large Apothekenhof (Apothecary Courtyard) behind the Festsaalbau, the Puderhöfchen (Small

Powder Courtyard), the Küchenhof (Kitchen Courtyard), the Kabinettsgarten (Cabinet Garden), and then finally the Zierhöfchen (Decorative Courtyard or Comité Courtyard).

The inner view of the Residenz museum

The galleries, the portraits, paintings, jewellery, and decorations of various halls and rooms are absolutely beautiful. Ideally, it takes almost 5 hours to see this museum in detail. We could see the museum for almost 3 hours and it was their closing time by the time we were out of the museum. Then our next visit was to the BMW welt. There are the latest models and technologies displayed for the public to view and experience the world of the upcoming technologies. We could not visit the museum which was near to the welt. Then very close to it was the Olympic Park and the tower. We went to the tower and could see the Olympic stadium and the residential complex built for sportsmen and have a good view of Munich city. On the evenings of the first day and the second day, we were in the city centre sprawling the streets. Some more information about the area is therefore given to know. On the way through the pedestrian mall, we could see the green building complex of the Munich police headquarters to the left on Ettstraße. Many people have come to know about this structure through the Munich "Tatort" TV series. The headquarters accommodates the Polizeimuseum which is open to the public.

The inner view of the Residenz museum   The BMW Museum

Inside the BMW welt

The exhibition documents police work, including spectacular police operations e.g. during the murderous attacks at the 1972 Olympics, and criminal cases such as the murder of the Munich fashion czar Rudolph Moshammer in 2005. A few steps farther on the left you get a view of Frauenkirche which was built by Jörg von Halsbach in the 15th century. The towers with the so-called "Welsh domes" are a landmark of the city. It is less known that the domes were designed according to the Dome of the Rock in Jerusalem, one of the most important sanctuaries of Islam. The Twin Towers time and again inspire spectacular feats. In 1935 the devilish pilot Ernst Udet roared his plane between the two towers by flying sideways. In 2014 a large-scale police operation was required to stop extreme climbers who had already mounted the southern tower up to the belfry. After extensive renovation work, the southern tower can be visited again. The next place is the Marienplatz. At the time of Munich's foundation in 1158 the whole settlement was not much larger than this square. St. Mary's Column (Mariensäule) in the middle of the square gave the former marketplace its name. It dates back to an oath taken during the Thirty Years War when Munich was occupied but not destroyed by the Swedes. The Neue Rathaus is the office of the Lord Mayor. From its balcony, the FC Bayern Munich greets its fans at championship celebrations. At 11 am and noon (and in summer also at 5 pm), numerous spectators watch the Carillon (Glockenspiel) in the town hall tower. On the ground level of the town hall, the city's Tourist Information provides advice to visitors. Munich hosted the 1972 Summer Olympics. After winning the bid in 1966 the Mayor of Munich Hans-Jochen Vogel accelerated the construction of the U-Bahn subway and the S-Bahn metropolitan commuter railway. In May 1967 the construction work began for a new U-Bahn line connecting the city with the Olympic Park. The Olympic Park subway station was built near the BMW Headquarters which we used for reaching the BMW welt and also the Olympic tower, and the line was completed in May 1972, three months before the opening of the 1972 Summer Olympics. Shortly before the opening ceremony, Munich also inaugurated a sizable pedestrian priority zone between Karlsplatz and Marienplatz. In 1970 the Munich city council released funds so that the iconic gothic facade and Glockenspiel of the New City Hall (Neues Rathaus) could be restored. There are many more things in the city center, the photos of which are given in the text. The information about these places is available online. Thus our Munich city visit was over.

NUREMBURG

18th May Saturday, we were to go to Nuremburg. We started from our hotel in the morning and reached the Munich HBF to take train RE1. We don't know why but the trains were cancelled and rescheduled resulting in a very heavy rush in the train. We somehow could get onto the train with our luggage and were almost standing till the time we reached Nuremburg HBF. We met a student from Pune, Mr Amey Kale who with his family was staying in Munich and travelling to Nuremberg from there to another place. Since there was ample time we could talk about the DB services, the culture, the food habits, and many things we could discuss. He helped us get into the train in the heavy rush. He said that there is maintenance work due to which these types of problems do come.

St Lawrence Church

The Beautiful fountain

We reached Nuremberg at about 1.30 PM. And the hotel was within walking distance. We checked into our room and asked the receptionist how we should see the city. The receptionist just gave us a map and told us to take a road from the hotel which, would reach the Nuremberg fort. All the things to see are along the road and we could take any path which is suitable for walking.

Tugendbrunnen

Narrenschiffbrunnen

The Church near the Rathaus

The Bimmelbahn train

Nuremberg (Nürnberg), Bavaria's second-largest city and the unofficial capital of Franconia, is an energetic place where the nightlife is intense and the beer is as dark as coffee. As one of Bavaria's biggest draws it is alive with visitors year-round, but especially during the spectacular Christmas market. The first tower that we saw was the Handwarkerhof. From there we came to the city and the next place that we could see was the St Lawrence church. We were along the King's strass.

The imperial Forte   St. Sebald Church

It is an old church with sculptures along the walls and the front side. Then we reached the Museum Bridge which has historical importance. We could see the Tugendbrunnen and Narrenschiffbrunnen on the way. Then we reached the city centre. Many local products were on sale in a local market in the city center. It was open only till 6 PM. And there was quite a rush in the area. We could see the beautiful fountain at the centre of this area. Then we walked between the Rathaus and the St Sebald Church towards the fort. The fortification of this fort has 3 layers and accordingly, the fortification is large enough for the kings to stay safe inside. We walked along the Burg Strass to reach the imperial castle. To this day, the city's skyline is dominated by the mighty fortress built in around 1140 during the reign of Emperor Konrad III. Nuremberg's historical mile ends (or begins) at the castle and features ornately decorated churches, elaborate fountains, and the Tucherschloss Museum. In stark contrast, other sites in Nuremberg serve only as necessary reminders of the darker years in the city's long history. They include the Documentation Centre at the former Nazi party rally grounds, where the National Socialists staged their vast marching processions, and Memorium Nuremberg Trials, where the chief perpetrators of the Nazi atrocities were tried and convicted in 1946. There are a lot of places to see inside the castle. There is a small museum and watch tower. We can see the fortification from all sides. After the fort, we chose an alternative route to reach the city centre. There were a few museums worth visiting but they were closed as we were late. When we reached the beautiful fountain we saw a small train called The Bimmelbahn train that would take us around the city for an hour's ride with a commentary. The train had 3 to 4 compartments. We enjoyed exploring the historic city of Nuremberg on board a picturesque tourist train, the Bimmelbhann train. Enjoy a ride through the city centre, departing from the main Market Square. Pass by the Schöner Brunnen, a beautiful 19-meter-high gold fountain. Next, drive by the Maxbrücke Bridge, St. Lawrence Church, the Hospital of the Holy Spirit, and the Imperial Castle, one of Europe's most important medieval fortifications. Enjoy panoramic views of all the sites visited from the comfort of your train seat. In addition, learn more about the history of the city and uncover its secrets and legends from your informative audio guide. During this tour, you will be able to see all of the city's highlights in just 40 minutes. The route covered almost all the important places that we could see. A good number of churches, bridges, the stages of fortification, etc. could be seen during this small journey. We could see the city of Nuremburg almost in half a day. After the tour, we were at the city's Hauptmarket, or "Main Market." Regarded as one of the top tourist attractions in Germany, Nuremberg has the unique distinction of having preserved most of its circuit of old city walls, many sections of which date from the 14th to 15th centuries, and later strengthened in the 16th and 17th centuries. The Germanic National Museum (Germanisches National Museum) is home to the country's largest collection related to German art and culture. Just outside the old town walls is the superb Nuremberg Transport Museum Overlooking Lorenzer Platz, the spectacular twin-towered 14th-century Gothic church of St. Lawrence (St. Lorenz, or Lorenzkirche) is the city's largest church. The Roman Catholic Frauenkirche (Church of Our Lady) dates back to 1352 and is a must-see Gothic landmark. Protestant St. Sebaldus Church (Sebalduskirche), built from 1225-73, boasts a magnificent Gothic east choir dating from 1379 featuring the Schreyer-Landauer tomb, the work of Adam Kraft. Just a stone's throw from Nuremberg Castle is the 15th-century Albrecht Dürer's House, The Documentation Centre. Nazi Party Rally Grounds (Dokumentationszentrum Reichsparteitagsgelände) is one of Germany's most important museums, dedicated to the bleakest chapters in the country's history. We could walk around different streets as it was broad daylight even until 8.30 PM. There were many small streets and they were converging to the main street. After walking around and reaching our hotel we had dinner and then rest. The next day we were to travel to Leipzig which is not very close and could take a lot of time to travel. Also, we had only that afternoon and evening to see the city of Leipzig. We had rest since we had got to be ready the next morning for the onward travel.

LEIPZIG

19th May, Sunday, we started from Nuremberg in the morning by train RE30 to Hof Hbf and with a crossover to RB13 to reach Leipzig. The Hotel at Leipzig was close to the HBF and we went walking. We checked in our room and asked the receptionist for the city map. The main monument in Leipzig is the Monument of the Battle of Nations. The Leipzig region was the arena of the 1813 Battle of Leipzig between Napoleonic France and an allied coalition of Prussia, Russia, Austria, and Sweden. It was the largest battle in Europe before the First World War and the coalition victory ended Napoleon's presence in Germany and would ultimately lead to his first exile on Elba. The Monument to the Battle of the Nations celebrating the centenary of this event was completed in 1913. In addition to stimulating German nationalism, the war had a major impact in mobilizing a civic spirit in numerous volunteer activities. Many volunteer militias and civic associations were formed and collaborated with churches and the press to support local and state militias, patriotic wartime mobilization, humanitarian relief, and post-war commemorative practices and rituals. The monument could be reached in about 20 Min. by tram from the city centre. The structure is 91 meters (299 ft) tall. It contains over 500 steps to a viewing platform at the top, from which there are views across the city and environs. The structure makes extensive use of concrete, and the facings are of granite. It is widely regarded as one of the best examples of Wilhelmine architecture. The monument is said to stand on the spot of some of the bloodiest fighting, from where Napoleon ordered the retreat of his army. The monument is quite big and there was some local festival and the ladies were wearing colored and decorated dresses with feathers, scarf, designs, and many more things. We were in the monument after taking the tickets. There is a big water tank in front of the monument and there are fountains around. There are lifts to take the tourists to various levels inside the monument. There are sculptures at various stages and we could see. There are light shows in the evening. The steps are through the walls and are quite steep. Fit persons can climb but the lifts are more advisable. There are sculptures at various stages depicting the war, soldiers, warriors, and other depictions. After visiting this sight we again used the tram to reach the city. When we discussed with the locals they said that the city can be easily covered by walking and would not require more than half a day. They were traveling in the same tram as we were. We left the tram at the opera house and the Augustasplatz.

Monument of the Battle of Nations.

Opera House Leipzig

Unzitgemase Zeitgenossen

Then we started walking towards the marketplace. On the way we could see Unzitgemase Zeitgenossen which are sculptures on the street arranged such that they can be seen from both directions. They have golden equipment in their hands or on their body. We then reached the market square, where there were large no of stalls, shops, restaurants, and the local crafts for display. After walking in that area we proceeded towards St. Thomas Church, Rathaus, and the new town hall. The Market in Leipzig, for many centuries the hub of city life, is dominated by the Old City Hall (Rathaus), a Renaissance building erected in 1556 and considered one of the most beautiful Renaissance buildings in Germany. Southwest of Leipzig's Market stands St. Thomas Church (Thomaskirche), home of the world-famous St. Thomas Boys' Choir. Built-in the 12th century, St. Nicholas Church (Nikolaikirche) has been altered in various ways over the centuries, the most recent transforming its interior into the Neoclassical style in the 1700s. Just opposite this hall, there was a big space where the celebrations and enjoyment were going on. All of this is in the city centre. Then we walked towards the famous University of Leipzig. The literary theorist Johann Gottsched was perhaps its most famous professor, and the mathematician Gottfried Leibniz, the literary figure Johann Wolfgang von Goethe, the philosopher Johann Fichte, and the composer Richard Wagner were students there. This university has many scholars as its aluminai. The campus is quite big and has a lot of different buildings and specialty departments. There was a heavy rush all along the road and in the area as it was a festival day. Everyone was in a festive mood.

Ladies with the Festival dress

Later we reached the Mendebrunnen which has a beautiful fountain at its centre. Immediately east of the University in Leipzig is the Gewandhaus, the magnificent home of the world-famous Gewandhaus Orchestra. Opposite one end of the Old City Hall is the entrance to the Mädlerpassage, one of the charming old shopping arcades that tunnel through buildings in the heart of the old city. One of the oldest coffee shops in Europe still in its original form, Coffe Baum opened in 1717. The Mendelssohn House in Leipzig is the only authentically preserved residence of the great composer, Felix Mendelssohn Bartholdy. In 1839 the first German railroad was opened between Leipzig and Dresden, and the accompanying growth of banks provided capital for the city's growing textile and metallurgical industries.   Leipzig is a major intellectual and cultural centre. The University of Leipzig dates from 1409. Leipzig has many museums, and its academies of dramatic art, musical history, graphic arts, and bookmaking are internationally known.

Mendebrunnen

The Market Square

Among the city's libraries are the German National Library and the Comenius Library, which is Europe's largest library specializing in education. The University Library, the Leipzig City Library, and the City Archives are also important. Musical traditions are carried on by the Thomaner Choir, the Gewandhaus Orchestra, and the Radio Symphony Orchestra. It was almost 9 PM. by the time we went around the city centre. We had dinner in the market area and returned to the hotel. We were walking back and near our hotel, there was a lady who was dressed in black and wearing the traditional attire. We requested a photo to which she willingly agreed and that is the photo included in this section. I must not forget to thank the ladies for the photographs in their festival and traditional dress. Since I don't know their names I cannot mention them but will certainly thank them.

BERLIN

20ᵗʰ May Monday. We were to travel to Berlin. We used the RE10 to Frankfurt Oder, got down at Doberlug-Kirchhain, took RE8 toward Berlin HBF and got down at Berlin Sudkreuz. We had discussed this route with Shruti and Sai, my friend's daughter and son-in-law respectively, who advised us to get down at Sudkreuz and use S Bahn to reach a stop close to the hotel. This was a stop before the Berlin HBF and it was near our hotel. From Sudkreuz we used the S Bahn S26 towards Blankenburg direction and after two stops we got down at Anhalterban and walked towards our hotel Holiday Inn Express Berlin city centre. We reached in the afternoon and the evening was free. In the evening it was our plan to go for dinner to Shruti Kuber's house as we were to give her sweets and a few other things which we had brought from our place. We were in touch with her for a long time. When she was in her home in Pune at my friend Umesh Kuber's house we had discussed a lot about the planning of the tour and she had also provided us with the 49 Euro Douchnbahn pass. During our online discussions, we discussed the Trains and other services that we can use, their timings, etc. After reaching the hotel we freshened up, called her and asked when we should reach her home. She said that both of them Sai and Shruti, were on holiday, so no problem with time. Her sister Rucha who also stays in Berlin, was also going to come for dinner and we all were to have dinner at her house. We used Google Maps to reach the S Bahn and to reach her home. As usual, google Maps, was not showing us the directions to walk towards her home so we had to call her and then her sister came to the station to take us to her home. With the sweets, we also followed the German Tradition to carry a wine bottle which we had bought in Leipzig. After reaching her home we relaxed and had very good discussions regarding our further travel plan and also what we had already visited. We were almost at half the stage of our travel by the time we had reached Berlin. We had the experience of a few cities and were to explore a few more. Umesh was also going to come to Berlin in June, we even discussed about his visit to Berlin. We had a good dinner and then using the S Bahn service reached our hotel to take rest. The next day was to start with a visit to the Reichstag, the visit to which we had booked about a month earlier. We reached the venue well in time and after the security, we were in the building. The building is a modern design from inside while the old fort-like structure is maintained. With a structure where most of the natural light is properly directed inside the building. We were seated in the spectator galleries just above the parliament house. We visited the parliament house and we were given a talk on its construction, during the cold war, the initial palace building, the history, and other details.

The Reichstag dome

Reichstag from inside

View from the Riechestag

The Inside view from the Reichstag

The Neo-Renaissance building was constructed between 1884 and 1894 in the Tiergarten district on the left bank of the River Spree to plans by the architect Paul Wallot. It housed both the Reichstag legislature of the German Empire and the Reichstag of the Weimar Republic. The Reich's Federal Council also originally met there. The building was initially used by the Reichstag for Nazi Germany, but severe damage in the Reichstag fire of 1933 prevented further use and the Reichstag moved to the nearby Kroll Opera House. The 1933 fire became a pivotal event in the entrenchment of the Nazi regime.

The Brandenburg Gate

Top of Brandenburg gate

The building underwent further damage during the Second World War and its symbolism made it an important target for the Red Army during the Battle of Berlin. After the war, the building was modernized and restored in the 1960s and used for exhibitions and special events, as its location in West Berlin prevented its use as a parliament building by either of the two Germanys. From 1995 to 1999, the Reichstag was fundamentally redesigned by Norman Foster for its permanent use as a parliament building in the now-<u>reunified</u> Germany. The keys were handed over to the President of the Bundestag, Wolfgang Thierse, on 19 April 1999. The Bundestag has been meeting there ever since. A landmark of the city is the walk-in glass dome above the plenary chamber, designed by Gottfried Böhm. In 1956, after some debate, the West German government decided that the Reichstag should not be torn down, but be restored instead under the guidance of Paul Baumgarten. The cupola of the original building, which had also been heavily damaged in the war, was dismantled, and the outside façade was made simpler with the removal of ornaments and statues. Reconstruction started in 1961 and was complete by 1971. During the reconstruction, the building was first almost completely gutted, taking out everything except the outer walls, including all changes made by Baumgarten in the 1960s. Respect for the historic aspects of the building was one of the conditions stipulated to the architects, so traces of historical events were to be retained in a visible state.

Altes Museum

The Egyptian collection

Among them were bullet holes and graffiti left by Soviet soldiers after the final battle for Berlin in April–May 1945. However, graffiti considered offensive was removed, in agreement with Russian diplomats at the time. Reconstruction was completed in 1999, with the Bundestag convening there officially for the first time on 19 April of that year. The Reichstag is now the second most visited attraction in Germany, not least because of the huge glass dome that was erected on the roof as a gesture to the original 1894 cupola, giving an impressive view over the city, especially at night. The large glass dome at the very top of the Reichstag has a 360° view of the surrounding Berlin cityscape.

The Reichstag building

The Brandenburg gate

The main hall (debating chamber) of the parliament below can also be seen from inside the dome, and natural light from above radiates down to the parliament floor. A large sun shield tracks the movement of the sun electronically and blocks direct sunlight which would not only cause large solar gain but dazzle those below.

Berlin Cathedral

The Berlin wall

Construction work was finished in 1999 and the seat of parliament was transferred to the Bundestag in April of that year. The dome is open to visitors by prior registration. Since we had booked the visit well in advance we could visit the entire area. During the visit we could see the inner structure modernized but the outer structure in the old glory. After the lecture, we had to give back our tourist pass and then take an elevator to the top of the building and then walk along the stairs to a top point on the Reichstag. The entire Berlin city could be viewed from the top. The glass structure is such that during the parliament session the spectators can see its functioning while not being visible to the persons inside the house. A lot of natural light enters inside and is used beautifully to control the temperature inside the Reichstag. Four square pillars are on four sides of the complex with flags representing the different regions. The large glass dome at the very top of the Reichstag has a 360° view of the surrounding Berlin cityscape. The main hall of the parliament below can also be seen from inside the dome, and natural light from above radiates down to the parliament floor. The visit lasted about 2 to 3 hours and then we went into the city to look for other attractions. From the Reichstag, we went to a garden just opposite to it. There was a war memorial with a little pond inside the garden. Then we reached the main attraction of Berlin which is the Brandenburg Gate which is close to the Reichstag. The Brandenburg Gate is located in the western part of the city centre within Mitte, at the junction of Unter den Linden and Ebertstraße. The gate dominates the Pariser Platz to the east, while to the immediate west, it opens onto the Platz des 18. One block to the north stands the Reichstag building, home to the German parliament (*Bundestag*), and further to the west is the Tiergarten inner-city park.

A Painting inside the art gallery

The Boating in the river spree

The gate also forms the monumental entry to Unter den Linden, which leads directly to the former City Palace of the Prussian monarchs (now housing the Humboldt Forum museum), and the Berlin Cathedral. Throughout its existence, the Brandenburg Gate was often a site for major historical events. After World War II and during the Cold War, until its fall in 1989, the gateway was obstructed by the Berlin Wall and was for almost three decades a marker of the city's division. Since German reunification in 1990, it has been considered not only a symbol of the tumultuous histories of Germany and Europe but also of European unity and peace. As planned we had some photographs there and then we bought the Berlin museum pass. The Berlin museum pass is a three-day pass and considering the number of museums and things to see the pass is worth its cost. The main street from Brandenburg gate to the Tiergarten was closed due to some maintenance work. There is a big column at the other end of the street which we could see from the distance. The first place that we thought of visiting was the museum island, where there are 4 to 5 museums along the bank of the river. We used suitable S Bahn to reach the museum island. The Museum Island is so-called for the complex of internationally significant museums, all part of the Berlin State Museums, that occupy the Spree island's northern part. In 1999, the museum complex was added to the UNESCO list of World Heritage Sites because of its unique testimony to the evolution of museums as a social and cultural phenomenon and the corresponding development of museum architecture. The Altes Museum (Old Museum) was named the *Königliches Museum* when it was built on 3 August 1830, until it was renamed in 1841. The museum was completed on the orders of Karl Friedrich Schinkel.

A painting in the art gallery   The roof of a museum

This museum was closed on the day we visited. But on the next day, we could see the vast collection of artefacts inside. There are a lot of different types of sculptures, photos, paintings and other things inside. The Neues Museum (New Museum) finished in 1859 according to plans by Friedrich August Stüler, a student of Schinkel. Destroyed in World War II, it was rebuilt under the direction of David Chipperfield for the Egyptian Museum of Berlin and re-opened in 2009. Fortunately, this museum was open on the day we visited the island. We could see the two interconnected museums, one museum had the elephant as its theme when we visited. There are lot of Egyptian artefacts inside the museum. The Alte Nationalgalerie (Old National Gallery) was completed in 1876, also according to designs by Friedrich August Stüler, to host a collection of 19th-century art donated by banker Joachim H. W. Wagener. This museum was open but there was an exhibition that was not included in the museum pass and therefore we could not visit this museum on the first day. But on the next day, there was a rush at this museum. The exhibitions of the paintings were really a beauty to watch. The Bode Museum on the island's northern tip opened in 1904 and was then called *Kaiser-Friedrich-Museum*. It exhibits the sculpture collections and late Antique and Byzantine art. This museum also we could see on the next day. This museum has an antique collection of porcelain, ornaments, silver, and other artifacts. This also has decorated rooms and halls which were used in the olden days.   The Pergamon Museum which was constructed in 1930 is presently closed to visitors.

Alte Nationalgallarie

The Rotes Rathous

It could be open after about 1 or 2 years for the public, as informed by the persons there. But they have a small museum just opposite this museum which has a small collection and a three-dimensional model of the historical events. The original museum contains multiple reconstructed immense and historically significant buildings such as the Pergamon Altar and the Ishtar Gate of Babylon. The Berliner Dom while not itself a museum is a historically important church, which contains the dynastic crypt of the House of Hohenzollern. The Lustgarten Park, The James Simon Gallery, visitors centre, opened in 2019. Since this was not included in the museum pass we could not see this church from inside. There was a beautiful garden in this area just in front of the church called Lust Garden. There are fountains and children's play areas while the visitors and locals can relax on the lawns. Nearby there is the Humboldt Forum opened in late 2020 in the reconstructed Berlin Palace opposite the Berliner Dom and Lustgarten Park and incorporated the Ethnological Museum of Berlin and the Museum of Asian Art, both are successor institutions of the Ancient Prussian Art Chamber, which was also located in the Berlin Palace and which was established in the mid 16th century. In late 2022, the opening of the eastern wing, the last section of the Humboldt Forum Museum, meant the Humboldt Forum Museum was finally completed. It is a big area inside and there are many programs, events, and functions going on inside the complex. Another museum just on the other bank of the river is the German Historical Museum, in the historic Zeughaus, including an extension by I. M. Pei, which is located opposite Lustgarten Park, just off the Island, along the Unter den Linden

Indian Monument near the Humboldt forum

A statue near Alte Nationalgallarie

Sculpture at the Berlin Wall Memorial

The Berlin Wall

After visiting this museum we were in the lust garden as on that day the other museums were closed. We could visit the Berlin Cathedral which is a beautiful and big cathedral. From there we went towards the Humboldt forum, St Nikolas church, the old market area, Rotes Rathaus, Fonte the Neptuno, St Mary Church, the Berlin TV tower, and Marks Engles forum which is in the Alexanderplatz area. By the time we were near the Humboldt forum, Shruti Kuber who has her university and also her workplace in this area, joined us and hence we could walk through the area and see many things mentioned. It was already 8 PM and hence dinner time. Since experiencing a beer garden in Germany is a must, after discussing it with her we decided to go to a beer garden by using the bus. The bus route was through the Brandenburg gate area and along the southern side of the Bundesstrass. The Bundesstrass was closed for maintenance. We could see the Indian Embassy along the road and reached the area of Pestana Burlin Tiergarten. Then by walking, we reached the place called café am Neuen See. This place is near a lake in the garden. There are benches all along and a facility of small self-driven boats that can be enjoyed. We did not do it but many were enjoying it. We had the famous pizza and local food and then traced the path to our hotel. We used public transport efficiently to reach the destination. The next day we went to visit the museums as already mentioned, but the famous Berlin Wall was the first thing we visited. There is a small museum near the wall. There are many things near the wall. The idea of a memorial was suggested by the Deutsches Historisches Museum (German Historical Museum) on behalf of the federal government of Berlin, and architects Kohlhoff & Kohlhoff were commissioned to design it. The cost of the competition and completion was 2.2 million Marks. The federal government took over the construction costs, while the state covered the maintenance costs. On 11 September 2008, the Berlin House of Representatives approved the opening of the memorial on the anniversary of the day that the Berlin Wall fell. By 2013, an extension was to be completed. Original relics of the border were to be shown, with missing parts marked in steel on the ground. The memorial was to be divided into four areas, The wall and the Todesstreifen (death strip), Destruction of the city, Building of the wall, and "Es geschah an der Mauer" ("It happened at the wall"). The documentation centre is located on the other side of Bernauer Straße. It contains seminar rooms and exhibitions. The building includes a five-story observation tower. At the corner of Gartenstraße and Bernauer Straße, a visitor centre was opened. The outdoor area of the memorial west of Berlin Nordbahnhof was transformed into an Erinnerungslandschaft (memorial landscape). In 2006 there were over 220,000 visitors to the documentation centre, which is part of the memorial. Part of the memorial is located on Ackerstraße. We were there for some time watching the photos and how the wall was brought down. From there we took the transport to the

Museum Island and visited the Bode Museum, a three-storied museum with many antique collections. Then very close to it is a very big museum which is temporarily closed and will open after 2 to 3 years. But just opposite to it a small space has been developed as the Pergamon Museum where there are three-dimensional depictions and some sculptures. Then we walked to the Altes museum which houses a collection of antiques, portraits, paintings, jewellery etc.

The Jews Memorial   A statue from Berlin Innenstadt park.

Then we went to the Alte National Gallery. This is a place where there is a collection of a lot of paintings. We enjoyed the exhibition. It was a nice collection. By the time it was almost 6 PM. By taking suitable transport we again went to the Brandenburg gate and visited a few places that we had not visited earlier, like the Jewish memorial, Potsdamer Platz, and checkpoint Charlie. The Jewish memorial is located in Cora-Berliner-Straße, a city with one of the largest Jewish populations in Europe before the Second World War. Adjacent east to the Tiergarten, it is centrally located in Berlin's historical Friedrichstadt district, close to the Reichstag building and the Brandenburg Gate.[9] The monument is situated on the former location of the Berlin Wall, where the "death strip" once divided the city. During the Third Reich, a part of this area was the location of Joseph Goebbels's urban villa, with the nearby Reich Chancellery and the Führerbunker in the south. The memorial is located near many of Berlin's foreign embassies. The monument is composed of 2,711 rectangular concrete blocks, laid out in a grid formation, the monument is organized into a rectangle-like array covering 1.9 hectares (4 acres 3 roods). This allows for long, straight, and narrow alleys between them, along which the ground undulates. From there we went to the Checkpoint Charlie. Checkpoint Charlie was a crossing point in the Berlin Wall located at the junction of Friedrichstraße with Zimmerstraße and Mauerstraße (which for older historical reasons coincidentally means "Wall Street"). It is in the Friedrichstadt neighborhood. Checkpoint Charlie was designated as the single crossing point (on foot or by car) for foreigners and members of the Allied forces. Members of the Allied forces were not allowed to use the other sector crossing point designated for use by foreigners, the Friedrichstraße railway station. As the most visible Berlin Wall checkpoint, Checkpoint Charlie was featured in movies and books. A famous cafe and viewing place for Allied officials, armed forces, and visitors alike, Cafe Adler ("Eagle Café"), was situated right at the checkpoint. Potsdamer Platz is a public square and traffic intersection in the centre of Berlin, Germany, lying about 1 km (1,100 yard) south of the Brandenburg Gate and the Reichstag (German Parliament Building), and close to the southeast corner of the Tiergarten Park. It is named after the city of Potsdam, some 25 km (16 mi) to the southwest, and marks the point where the old road from Potsdam passed through the city wall of Berlin at the Potsdam Gate. Initially, the open area near the city gate was used for military drills and parades. In the 19th into 20th centuries, it developed from an intersection of suburban thoroughfares into the most bustling traffic intersection in Europe. The area was totally destroyed during World War II and then left desolate during the Cold War era when the Berlin Wall bisected its location. Since German reunification, Potsdamer Platz has been the site of major redevelopment projects. Thus we had covered a lot of places that are included in the Berlin Pass. Of course, we could not visit all the museums and also all the must-see places but we had covered most of it. The next day we were to visit the Potsdam.

On the next day, after breakfast, we took the bus from the hotel to reach the Berlin HBF and then used the RE trains to reach Potsdam. It takes about 1 hour to reach Potsdam. It is well connected with Berlin. After we reached we were approached by a hop-on hop-off bus agent. He asked us to book the bus and go around the city. We usually use the local transport but this time we used the hop-on-hop-off bus. The historic city of Potsdam, the capital of the state of Brandenburg, is located just 40 kilometers southwest of Berlin. Potsdam is the capital and largest city of the German state of Brandenburg. It is part of the Berlin/Brandenburg Metropolitan Region. Potsdam sits on the River Havel, a tributary of the Elbe, downstream of Berlin, and lies embedded in a hilly Morainic landscape dotted with many lakes, around 20 of which are located within Potsdam's city limits. It lies some 25 kilometers (16 miles) southwest of Berlin's city centre. The name of the city and many of its boroughs are of Slavic origin. Potsdam was a residence of the Prussian kings and the German Emperor until 1918. Its planning embodied ideas of the Age of Enlightenment, through a careful balance of architecture and landscape, Potsdam was intended as "a picturesque, pastoral dream" that would remind its residents of their relationship with nature and reason. The city, which is over 1,000 years old, is widely known for its palaces, its lakes, and its overall historical and cultural significance. Landmarks include the parks and palaces of Sanssouci, Germany's largest World Heritage Site, as well as other palaces such as the Orangery Palace, the New Palace, Cecilienhof Palace, and Charlottenhof Palace. Potsdam was also the location of the significant Potsdam Conference in 1945, the conference where the three heads of government of the USSR, the US, and the UK decided on the division of Germany following its surrender, a conference that defined Germany's history for the following 45 years. Later, the city became a full residence of the Prussian royal family. The buildings of the royal residences were built mainly during the reign of Frederick the Great. One of these is the Sanssouci Palace, famed for its formal gardens and Rococo interiors. Other royal residences include the New Palace and the Orangery. In 1815, at the formation of the Province of Brandenburg, Potsdam became the provincial capital until 1918, except for a period between 1827 and 1843 when Berlin was the provincial capital. The province comprised two governorates named after their capitals Potsdam and Frankfurt (Oder). The Cecilienhof Palace was the scene of the Potsdam Conference from 17 July to 2 August 1945, at which the victorious Allied leaders Harry S. Truman, Winston Churchill, and Joseph Stalin met to decide the future of Germany and post-war Europe in general. The conference ended with the Potsdam Agreement and the Potsdam Declaration. After German reunification, Potsdam became the capital of the newly re-established state of Brandenburg. Since then there have been many ideas and efforts to reconstruct the original appearance of the city, including the Potsdam City Palace and the Garrison Church. Potsdam was historically a centre of European immigration. Its religious tolerance attracted people from France, Russia, the Netherlands, and Bohemia. This is still visible in the culture and architecture of the city. The most popular attraction in Potsdam is Sanssouci Park, 2 km west of the city centre. In 1744 King Frederick the Great ordered the construction of a residence here, where he could live sans souci ("without worries"). The park hosts a botanical garden (Botanical Garden, Potsdam) and many buildings, The Sanssouci Palace (Schloss Sanssouci), a relatively modest palace of the Prussian royal (and later German imperial) family, The Orangery Palace (Orangerieschloss), former palace for foreign royal guests, The New Palace (Neues Palais), built between 1763 and 1769 to celebrate the end of the Seven Years' War, in which Prussia held off the combined attacks of Austria and Russia. It is a much larger and grander palace than Sanssouci, having over 200 rooms and 400 statues as decoration. It served as a guest house for numerous royal visitors. Today, it houses parts of the University of Potsdam. The Charlottenhof Palace (Schloss Charlottenhof), a Neoclassical palace by Karl Friedrich Schinkel built in 1826. The Roman Baths (Römische Bäder), built by Karl Friedrich Schinkel and Friedrich Ludwig Persius in 1829–1840. It is a complex of buildings including a tea pavilion, a Renaissance-style villa, and a Roman bathhouse, from which the whole complex takes its name. The Chinese Tea House (Chinesisches Teehaus), is an 18th-century pavilion built in a Chinese style, the fashion of the time. Three gates from the original city wall remain today. The oldest is the Hunters' Gate (Jägertor), built in 1733. The Nauener Tor was built in 1755 and is close to the historic Dutch Quarter. The ornate Brandenburg Gate, built in 1770, not to be confused with the Brandenburg Gate in Berlin is situated on the Luisenplatz at the western entrance to the old town. As one of Germany's most famous former imperial cities, this beautiful travel destination makes for a splendid day trip from the capital. The bus went through the city centre covering the old city, its buildings, streets, etc. We could see the famous Glienicker Bridge which was the place where the change of guards used to take place. One side of the bridge was the Russian part and the other was British or American.

Orangery Palace

Sans Souci palace

Then we visited a palace where the meeting regarding the end of the Cold War and the unification of Germany was held. Then we went towards the new palace. There were several palaces on the way. We left the hop-on hop-off bus at the new palace and then took the tickets to visit the new palace. There was a group that we were supposed to join and then we were shown about 38 rooms inside the palace which were a beauty to visit.

Obilisk

Inside the New Palace

There was a marble room, the meeting rooms, the jewellery and many more things. After seeing the palace we visited the royal garden which is part of the royal estate which is the Sanssouci Park, home to many exquisite gardens, impressive buildings, artworks, and walking trails. Established in 1744, the park's highlights include Neptune's Grotto and the Picture Gallery. Housed in the Orangery, this impressive art collection, with its collection of 17th-century paintings, including works by Rubens, van Dyck, and Caravaggio, is a must-see. Also of note in the palace grounds is the Great Fountain which has the four elements and mythological figures.

The New Palace   The New palace

After walking in the garden we reached the end point of the garden where there is a column called Obilisk. From there we again picked the bus to reach the HBF from where we returned to Berlin. We reached Berlin at about 8.00 PM. We had dinner and reached our hotel to take a rest.

HAMBURG

On the next day, we were to go to Hamburg for which we chose the bus from our hotel as this would reduce the baggage transport to a good extent. We reached HBF and then we used the train RE8 to Wismer and got own at Schwerin Hbf, this was a very small station. We just had to cross the track and wait for the train to arrive. The train was late by almost one hour and since there was no roof we were in the open platform. After the train arrived which was RE1 towards Hamburg. We reached Hamburg in the afternoon at about 2 PM. The hotel in Hamburg was Hotel Wilhelm Busch for which we used the U Bahn to reach Ochsenzoll HBF and the Bus to reach the hotel. After reaching the hotel and getting fresh we were in the city using the same U Bahn route and reached the city centre getting down at Jungfernstieg HBF.

Hamburg Townhall

Hamburg Townhall

Hamburg is a city, and *Land* (state), located on the Elbe River in northern Germany. It is the country's largest port and commercial centre. The Free and Hanseatic City (Freie und Hansestadt) of Hamburg is the second smallest of the *16* Länder of *Germany*, with a territory of only 292 square miles (755 square km). It is also the most populous city in Germany after Berlin and has one of the largest and busiest ports in Europe. The official name, which covers both the *Land* and the town, reflects Hamburg's long tradition of particularism and self-government. Hamburg and Bremen (the smallest of the Länder) are, in fact, the only German city-states that still keep something of their medieval independence. The characteristic individuality of Hamburg has been proudly maintained by its people so that, in many spheres of public and private life, the city's culture has retained its uniqueness and has not succumbed to the general trend of standardization. Among Hamburg's many other facets are a network of canals reminiscent of Amsterdam; lakes, parks, and verdant suburbs full of gracious houses; elegant shopping arcades; richly endowed museums; and a vibrant cultural life. These are among the attractions that have contributed to a growing tourist industry. Although it was badly damaged during World War II, Hamburg has succeeded in maintaining a sense of old-world grace alongside its thriving commercial life.

Inside the Hamburg Townhall

St. Nikolai Memorial

The last intact ensemble of traditional Hamburg architecture is to be found in the Deichstrasse, one side of which backs onto the Nikolai canal. Its tall, narrow houses, resembling those of Amsterdam, were originally built from the 17th through the 19th century. It was in one of them, number 42, now a restaurant, that the devastating fire of 1842 broke out. Afterward the houses were rebuilt in the old style. Today the street is a protected area, and in recent years it has undergone extensive restoration. Many traditional restaurants are found there. Another survival of older architecture is in the Krameramtswohnungen, near Sankt Michaelis. Consisting of two half-timbered brick buildings on either side of a narrow courtyard, it was built as a series of dwellings for the widows of shopkeepers and is the only surviving 17th-century construction of its kind in the city. Thoroughly restored between 1971 and 1974, it now forms a delightful secluded alleyway housing a restaurant, small shops, and a branch of the Museum für Hamburgische Geschichte (Museum of Hamburg History). Of Hamburg's five great churches, the most imposing is probably Sankt Michaelis, an 18th-century Baroque-style Protestant church with a rich white-and-gold interior. It was destroyed by fire in 1906, rebuilt, devastated again during World War II, and restored yet again after the war. The prosperous years 1890–1910 brought an abundance of fine architecture, examples of which can be seen in the spacious and elegant patrician houses around the Aussenalster. Many of these are now occupied by consulates. Another period of architectural flowering came in the 1920s and 1930s when there was a revival of the use of the traditional north German dark red brick as a building material, led by the architects Fritz Höger and Fritz Schumacher.

Neue Burg

The water channels in the city

A good example is Höger's Chilehaus, a massive office building constructed between 1922 and 1924. More recently Hamburg has acquired its quota of starkly functional modern buildings, such as the Congress Centrum (Congress Centre; opened 1973) and the Fernsehturm (Television Tower), 271.5 metres (891 feet) high, but there is now a strong tendency to renovate old houses rather than to demolish and build afresh. Thus the townscape of Hamburg as a whole has a human quality lacking in many German cities. The magnificent Rathaus (City Hall), where the Senate and the Bürgerschaft meet, in the centre of the city near the Binnenalster, was built late in the 19th century in the Neo-Renaissance style. Hamburg's coat of arms displays a three-towered castle, intended to represent the Hammaburg, silver (argent), on a red (gules) field, its design being derived from the city's great seal of 1241. The state flag likewise shows a white castle on a red field. The state's anthem, "Stadt Hamburg an der Elbe Auen" ("City of Hamburg by the Meadows of the Elbe"), was written by G.N. Bärmann in 1828 and set to music by Albert Methfessel.

Elbphilharmonie

Alter Albetunnel

After reaching the city centre just outside the station, we saw the Hamburg Townhall. We got inside the town hall and saw the beautiful inner structure, portraits, paintings, etc. The Alster fountain was just across the road. Then we went to the St. Nikolai Memorial, where was a lift to the top of the church tower with a ticket, we could observe a good view of the city from the top. Close to it, there was the St. Nikolai Museum included in the same ticket. The museum had pictures and information about the destruction of the city during WWII and the way it was rebuilt. There was Neue Burg just in front of it. Then close to it was the Hopfenmarkt. The entire area has a large number of water channels and a large number of bridges that we cross during the walk in this area. Elbphilharmonie is a special attraction of Hamburg. It is a concert hall with new glassy construction that resembles a hoisted sail, water wave, and iceberg-like structure. It has the old brick structure at the bottom on which the glassy structure is developed. The concert hall was opened to the public during the year 2017. We could see the structure and enjoy the views of the area. The area has a lot of warehouses and water channels. Some cruises take us around the port area. Even though the open sea is far the big vessels, used for trading come very close to the harbour area. Then we walked towards the Hafencity and the University area and then returned back to the city centre to have dinner. After dinner, we used the U Bahn to reach the hotel.

The next we started from our hotel after breakfast and we were on the bus near to our hotel. We could see the local persons with different types of coloured dress and their attire was festive attire. When we asked them they said that there was a festival in the city in the afternoon. Accordingly, we planned to see a few places in the city centre before this event, as the persons said that there would be a few lakh people in the festive event. After taking the U Bahn and reaching the city centre we first planned to visit the famous Elbe tunnel which is quite old and historically important.

Near the Hamburg Zoo

Near the Hamburg zoo

Old Elbe Tunnel or St. Pauli Elbe Tunnel, was opened in 1911, and is a pedestrian and vehicle tunnel in Hamburg. The 426 m (1,398 ft) long tunnel was a technical sensation, it is 24 m (80 ft) beneath the surface, and two 6 m (20 ft) diameter tubes connect central Hamburg with the docks and shipyards on the south side of the river Elbe. This was a big improvement for tens of thousands of workers in one of the busiest harbors in the world. Six large lifts on either side of the tunnel carry pedestrians and vehicles to the bottom. The two tunnels are both still in operation, though due to their limited capacity by today's standards, other bridges and tunnels have been built and taken over most of the traffic. We used the tunnel which was for walking and cyclists only. In the tunnel an art exhibition and a long-distance running event Elbtunnel-Marathon take place. In 2008 the tunnel participated in the Tag des offenen Denkmals which is the "Day of the Open Heritage Site", a Germany-wide annual event sponsored by the Deutsche Stiftung Denkmalschutz that opens cultural heritage sites to the public. On the occasion of the reopening of the east tube on May 22 and 23, 2019, the Hamburg University of Music and Drama and the Hamburg Port Authority organized 4 concerts "Symphony in the St. Pauli Elbtunnel" under the direction of Prof. Georg Hajdu. The pieces composed specifically for this space were orchestrated with strings, winds, accordion, percussion, and vocals. For each of the 144 musicians distributed in the two tunnel tubes, the music was displayed in real-time on tablets individually controlled by a server computer.

The crowed in the festival celebration   One couple for the festival

The enthusiastic audience walked through the tube and everyone had a unique, individual listening and sound experience in space and time. The tunnel walls are decorated with glazed terra cotta ornaments displaying items related to the Elbe river. While most show fish or crabs, a few show different items like litter and rats, too. To enter the tunnel we have to reach the Hamburg Landing Bridge area where there is an old structure that is now converted into a shopping area. The Elbe tunnel is close to this area and the entrance can be reached by walking across the shops and other places. We used the entrance at Alter Albe tunnel and walked down to the actual tunnel. The tunnel is very old and under the Elbe, the vessels and other water transport take place above the tunnel, so we can imagine the depth at which this tunnel is placed. Crossing the tunnel we reached the other side where there is an old Elbe tunnel viewpoint from where we can have a good view of the St Paulie Piers, and the other areas in the port area. We have to walk back from the viewpoint on the other side of the tunnel and then through the tunnel to reach the Alter Albe tunnel back. We could see people with coloured attire in this part also. After we came out and even in the tunnel we could see the festive mood and the people with colourful clothes. After this visit, we went to visit the famous zoo area. A Chinese garden is located there and the interior has a lot of variations. After visiting the zoo and seeing the different flora, fauna, reptiles, birds, and animals we came out of the zoo and then we went into the festival area. It was afternoon and the festive celebrations were to take place in the St. Paulies Piers we chose to go to the St. Paulies Piers. As we approached the area we witnessed the festival in full swing. There were trucks loaded with balloons and music systems, and all the people inside the truck and walking with the trucks were dancing and enjoying the event. The event is a colorful festival. It is a three-day event. Traditional dress and groups were performing on the music that they were used to. The estimated number of persons could be almost 5 lakhs. All the roads were filled with the public and full of enjoyment. After enjoying this we went back to the city centre and after visiting a few more places, we returned to the hotel. The next day we were on the way to our next destination, Cologne. The distance and the time required for the travel to Cologne was long and involved change of the trains three times.

COLOGNE

26th May 2024, Sunday. The trains were crowded and even though we changed trains three times there was a rush all along the route. We started from Hamburg in the morning after breakfast. From the hotel taking the bus and the U Bahn we reached the Hamburg HBF. We alighted from RE3 at Hannover, took RE70 to Minden West, and then RE6 to Cologne. After studying the route we found that it is better to get down one stop before Cologne HBF, it was Cologne Messe. After getting down there we were required to take a tram and bus to reach our hotel. We reached Cologne in the afternoon, since our hotel was on the eastern side of the river we decided to get off the train at Cologne Messe, take the tram and bus and reached our hotel, Holiday Inn Express Cologne Mulheim. It is not close to the city centre but accessible by bus and tram. It was already evening and going to the city centre and returning seemed to be a big task hence we had our dinner at the hotel and preferred to rest.

Cologne Cathedral

Inside the Cologne Cathedral

The next day we left the hotel after breakfast and using the tram reached the city centre. The Cologne cathedral is very close to the Cologne HBF. Cologne is the fourth largest city in Germany and the largest city of the Land (state) of North Rhine–Westphalia. One of the key inland ports of Europe, it is the historic, cultural, and economic capital of the Rhineland. Cologne Cathedral eclipses in its size and grandeur all other historic buildings in the city. Its twin towers rise 515 feet (157 meters) above the city centre. After an earlier cathedral on the site was destroyed by fire in 1248, it was decided that a new one would be built in the Gothic style, emulating the cathedrals of France.   The choir was completed in 1320 and consecrated in 1322. Construction continued until 1560, when it came to a halt. The cathedral stood unfinished until 1842, when work was resumed. In 1880 the enterprise was finally completed. The building was badly damaged by air raids in 1944, but by 1948 the choir had been restored and was again in regular use, as was the rest of the interior by 1956.

The Famous Cologne Bridge

The Buildings along the Rhine

Ongoing work is needed to repair the effects of acid rain on the cathedral's stonework. The 14th-century stained-glass windows in the choir are considered especially beautiful, and the cathedral is also noted for its other art treasures. On the high altar is a massive gold shrine containing what are said to be relics of the Magi, sent to Cologne from Milan in 1164. This shrine, begun by Nicholas of Verdun in 1182 and completed in about 1220, is considered one of the finest examples of medieval gold work. The altar in the Lady Chapel (on the south wall of the choir) has a triptych, The Adoration of the Magi, painted between about 1440 and 1445 by Stefan Lochner, an outstanding painter of the Cologne school. By the south side of the cathedral lies a reminder of

Cologne's still more ancient past, the mosaic floor of a banquet hall in a great Roman villa, discovered during excavations near the cathedral in 1941. The floor is now incorporated into the Roman and Germanic Museum. Other Roman remains in Cologne include a well-preserved 1st-century-CE tower from the earliest city wall, the remains of the North Gate, a large portion of the Praetorium visible in the basement of the restored Gothic Town Hall, and a mausoleum in Weiden on the outskirts. The Ubier Monument, discovered in the 1960s, dates from the period of the Ubii occupation of the area. Remains of the medieval walls can still be seen, and three of the original 12 gates survive, Eigelstein Gate, Hahnen Gate, and Severins Gate.

At the Market Square

Inside the Chocolate Factory

The medieval Bayen Tower stands near the Rhine. Among Cologne's secular medieval buildings that suffered in World War II and have undergone reconstruction are the Overstolzen House, a 13th-century Romanesque house, and the Town Hall, with its 16th-century porch. The Gürzenich, or Banquet Hall, of the merchants of the city (1441–47), reconstructed as a concert and festival hall, and the 16th-century Arsenal, which contains a historical museum, were both restored to their medieval form only on the outside. These ancient buildings share the crowded city centre with modern offices, shops, a theatre and opera house opened in 1957, and, just north of the cathedral, the railway station. Near the perimeter of the city is the new town hall. Located about a mile from the cathedral is the 798-foot (243-metre) Telecommunications Tower (1981). The city remains a banking centre, as it was in the Middle Ages, and it is the site of one of the world's oldest commodity and stock exchanges. It has been a centre of the automotive industry—notably engine manufacture—since the late 19th century and is now the headquarters of the European operations of the Ford Motor Company. But business activity has become greatly diversified. Insurance has assumed a major position, and Cologne is a leading media centre with many publishing houses and production companies for radio and television. Engineering, electrical engineering, machinery, chemicals, and pharmaceuticals also are significant. Other manufacturers include chocolate and the city's famous eau de cologne, which was first produced commercially at the beginning of the 18th century.

The Lindes Chocolate factory

The Claudius Therme

In addition, several prominent economic organizations have their headquarters in Cologne, and numerous major trade fairs are held annually in the KölnMesse. The Max Planck Institute for Plant Breeding Research is headquartered in the city. Cologne is rich in museums and galleries. These include the Wallraf-Richartz and Ludwig museum complex, with an exceptionally comprehensive collection ranging from paintings of the medieval Cologne school to contemporary art, the Schnütgen Museum of medieval ecclesiastical art, the Museum of Oriental Art, with artworks from China and Japan, and the Rautenstrauch-Joest Museum, with ethnological collections. The Roman and Germanic Museum houses artifacts from the period of the migrations of the Germanic peoples and that of the Roman occupation. Special exhibitions are held in the Josef-Haubrich Hall of Art exhibition centre near the Neumarkt. A city museum and museums of photography and chocolate are also notable. Cologne contains several important libraries, including the state archives. Cologne's commercial importance grew out of its position at the point where the huge traffic artery of the Rhine River intersected one of the major land routes for trade between Western and Eastern Europe. In the Middle Ages, it also became an ecclesiastical centre of significance and an important centre of art and learning. This rich and varied heritage is still much in evidence in present-day Cologne, despite the almost complete destruction of the Inner City (Innenstadt) during World War II. Cologne is the seat of a university and the seat of a Roman Catholic archbishop. Its cathedral, the largest Gothic church in northern Europe, was designated a UNESCO World Heritage site in 1996, it is the city's major landmark and unofficial symbol.

The Bruhl castle

I nside the Bruhl castle

Inside the cathedral, we saw the paintings, painted glasswork, sculptures and many more things. The city's towering landmark is located near the left bank of the Rhine, and there are museums close to the cathedral along the bank of the Rhine. We spent a little time exploring the Old Town's Archaeological Zone with its many ancient ruins and artifacts. These include the Roman-era ruins of the Praetorium, or Governor's Palace, that was unearthed under the City Hall, as well as a section of a nearly 2,000-year-old Roman sewage system. A particular highlight of the city's Old Town area is Cologne's historic City Hall, the Kölner Rathaus, or Stadt Köln. Built in 1573 and the oldest such public building in Germany, it boasts a rich history dating back more than 900 years. Then we were on the Hohenzollern bridge on which there were a huge number of locks. This bridge is also called a locks bridge. Considering the weight of the locks on the bridge the authorities have established a structure for the locks close to the Ludwik Museum. From there we walked towards the old market area, Rathaus, Heumarkt, then towards the river bank to reach the Chocolate Museum. It is a big museum, we can see the entire process of chocolate making right from the fruit to its drying, processing, mixing, shaping, and finishing. They even give sample chocolates inside and there are a lot of places inside where we can watch the entire process. It takes about 1 to 1.5 hours to visit this museum. When we were out of the museum, we were to cross a bridge called Drehbrucke im Rheinauhafen just opposite the museum. We were stopped there and had to wait for the bridge to turn towards the city a make way for a ferry boat to cross the channel created between the chocolate museum and the street road on the bank. This was the first time that such a mechanical movement of the bridge was witnessed by us. The bridge was restored again making way for all of us to cross the bridge. After visiting the chocolate factory we took a small city ride using a carriage which went through the entire city centre and returned. We saw many things during our travel like the Rheingarten, musical dome, and church of St. Ursula, Edith Steindenkmai, Romerturm, etc. We returned to the same point from where we had started. Later we were to ride a cable car across the Rhine. Since its establishment in 1957 as the first European cable car to cross a river – in this case, the Rhine – the Cologne cable car or Rhein-Seilbahn has carried millions of passengers. The views are, of course, a big draw, particularly those of the Old Town and Cologne Cathedral. The cable car could be taken after reaching the pickup point, which is the zoological garden close to the Rhine bank. We went to the zoological garden and had a beautiful ride across the Rhine. The cable car over the Rhine was opened on April 26, 1957 in time for the opening of the biannual German horticultural show, the Bundesgartenschau; it connects the exhibition sites at Rheinpark with those on the other riverside, close to Cologne Zoo and Flora/Botanical Garden. Amongst its first guests were the President of Germany, Theodor Heuss, and Federal Chancellor and former Mayor of Cologne, Konrad Adenauer. In 2010 in Koblenz, another aerial tram crossing the Rhine opened, because of the 2011 edition of the Bundesgartenschau. From 1957 to 2004 the cable car transported 13.7 million people without an accident and in 2004, it carried 288,500 passengers. It is considered to be Cologne's safest means of transport. Starting in 2004, the cable car ran at night for special occasions and since that year it has been profitable. Kölner Seilbahn operates the tramway, which since 1998 has been a subsidiary of the Kölner Verkehrs-Betriebe, the city's public transit operator. We could see the entire city from the elevated sight. When on the other side we could see the Claudius Therme and we planned to visit it. It seemed to be near the hotel. After the gondola ride was over we came again back to the city centre. We again walked around the cathedral area till it was almost 7 PM. We had our dinner and returned to the hotel.

Inside the Bruhl castle

The Bruhl Castle Garden   The Bruhl castle

The next day we first visited the Bruhl Palace about 15 KM from Cologne. We reached Bruhl in one and a half hours by train. In the picturesque town of Brühl, an easy 15-kilometer drive south of Cologne stands Schloss Augustusburg. The palace complex consists of the Augustusburg

Palace and the smaller Falkenlust Lodge roughly 1 mile to the southeast. The main block of Augustusburg Palace is a U-shaped building with three main stories and two levels of attics. The three wings are made of brick with a roughcast plaster. Two orangeries adjoin the main building on the north and south sides. The magnificent main staircase was designed by **Johann Balthasar Neumann** and made of ornate marble, jasper, and stucco. The main garden directly south of the Augustusburg Palace is a complex, embroidery-like parterre, with four fountains and a mirror pool, flanked by alleys lined with lime trees. A path runs diagonally south from this garden to the Falkenlust lodge. The Falkenlust lodge was built in the style of a country home, drawing inspiration from the Amalienburg hunting lodge in the park of Nymphenburg Palace. The main building has two floors, flanked by two single-story buildings that housed the prince-elector's falcons. On the ground floor is an oval salon. This elegant 18th-century palace is famous as the home of the Archbishop of Cologne. The palace is close to the HBF so we walked to the castle. The castle had a ticket and we joined the group which had just taken the tickets. It is a guided tour and therefore a group tour. We had the English translator given to us and we could see the palace from inside. It is a beautiful palace with different halls, drapery, jewellery, and ceramics with the roofs beautifully painted and decorated. The palace is near the city of Cologne and worth visiting. The garden in front of the palace is huge and has water fountains all around. It takes quite some time to take a walk around the garden. After visiting the palace and the garden we were back to the HBF from where we returned to Cologne. We again had a small walk around the city centre and returned to the hotel to visit the Claudius therma. The thermal mineral water of the Claudius Therme, a so-called "thermal sodium-chloride acidulant", is particularly suitable for bathing, but can also be drunk or inhaled. As a drinking cure, it relieves gastrointestinal complaints. As a spa cure, it helps with rheumatic complaints and intervertebral disc or joint diseases. It has a positive effect on high blood pressure, circulatory disorders, and stress diseases, activates enzymes, and stabilizes bone structure. The healthy spa effect of the unique thermal mineral water of the Claudius Therme is state-recognized. This exceptional water is, as effective as the thermal water of recognized health resorts, Healing for circulation, joints, intestines, and heart, Pure and natural, tested by Institut Fresenius, 39,000 years of underground flow through limestone and Dolomite rock, naturally enriched with minerals, Naturally carbonated, freshly extracted from deep rock layers with in-house wells. We reached the Claudius Therme taking a bus from the hotel. Since it was raining, we had to carry an umbrella. The bus has a special stop for this place. After we reached we enquired regarding the procedure to be followed. We were given the wristbands at the entrance from where we were supposed to enter the complex. We had our swimming costumes with us and then we entered the inner part. Claudius Therme in Cologne, Germany, offers a variety of pools and bathing options. Here's what you can find there, Thermal Pools - the main attraction. While there isn't a large swimming pool, there is one small pool (1.35 meters deep) with a unique shape that isn't ideal for swimming. Additionally, there are several bathtub-sized "pools" available. Jacuzzis- Enjoy warm, bubbling water in the jacuzzis, both indoors and outdoors. Cold Plunge Bath: For a refreshing experience, try the cold plunge bath. Saunas - Claudius Therme has various saunas, including a Finnish-style sauna. Remember that bathing suits are required in the thermal pools and bathing section, but not in the saunas and showers. There were 9 to 10 pools with different temperatures having bubbling and whirling facilities which massage the body. There was a sauna facility also. We were there for about 2 hours. When we had the hot water treatment and bath we came to the exit area. As we return the plastic coupon given to us while we entered, the scanning shows the amount of time spent inside and we are charged accordingly. There are changing and bath rooms in the exit area, and there are lockers to keep our belongings which can be locked with the same plastic ring given to us. We had to pay the charges and the minimum time for which charges are levied is 2 hrs. From there we returned to our hotel and had dinner and rest.

FRANKFURT

We had our breakfast and using the tram we reached the Cologne HBF. We started from Cologne by RE5 to reach Koblenz and from there by RE2 to reach Frankfurt. Since our hotel was near the airport we could get down at the airport HBF or Flughafen and use S8 to Offenbach and got down at Gateway Garden to reach Park Inn by Raddison which is close to the Airport or Flughafen. We reached in the afternoon and after check-in, we went to the city centre

St Pauls Church

The Iron footbridge

to see the tourist places in the city centre. We first reached the Hauptwache. Situated in the middle of the city and one of Frankfurt's busiest pedestrian areas, the Hauptwache, which literally translates as the "Main Guard," is famous for its mix of fine historic buildings and modern structures. The most notable building here is the old Baroque Guard House after which the square is named. Built-in 1730, it once housed the city's militia, a prison, and later, a police station, and now houses a café. A picturesque old imperial city on the River Main, Frankfurt am Main has long been an important commercial and economic centre. Frankfurt's impressive skyline is dominated by a great cluster of high-rise buildings in the banking quarter, giving it a distinct North American flavor, along with the nicknames "Manhattan" and "Chicago on the Main." Frequently ranked in the top 10 best cities in which to live and do business, this truly global city has also long been an important centre for cultural and tourism activities.

The Romerburg

Schirn Kunsthalle Frankfurt

Its huge trade fair complex, Messe Frankfurt, hosts important events such as the Frankfurt Book Fair (Frankfurter Buchmesse), the world's most important publishing event, along with internationally renowned music and cultural festivals. Frankfurt is also well known for its exceptional number of fine museums covering art, science, and history. It's also a lovely city to explore on foot, with many of these museums and attractions being within easy walking distance of the downtown core. If you do walk, be sure to include a stroll across the Main via the Eiserner Steg, a pedestrian footbridge originally built in 1911 and rebuilt since that links the Sachsenhausen district to the downtown core. Set in the heart of Frankfurt's Old Town (Altstadt), the Römerberg is an irregularly shaped square with the Justice Fountain (Gerechtigkeitsbrunnen) at its centre. Not only is it Frankfurt's most picturesque public square, it's the city's busiest pedestrian zone and home to numerous tourist attractions and fun things to do, including Christmas markets and other events. Points of interest here include its many open-fronted shops. Once common throughout the old town, and the Römer, this cluster of 11 historic buildings together made up the medieval-era Old Town Hall, Altes Rathaus. This popular Frankfurt attraction was faithfully reconstructed in 1954 from original 15th- to 18th-century floorplans. Of special note is the elegant Imperial Hall (Kaisersaal), once the scene of splendid banquets. Other notable buildings in the Römerberg include the New Town Hall, Neues Rathaus dating from 1908, the 14th-century Gothic Church of St. Leonhard; and St. Nicholas Church, with its carillon. Also of interest here is the Historical Museum, Historisches Museum Frankfurt. Founded in 1878, its interesting collections relate to Frankfurt's rich cultural history from medieval to modern times and the six traditional-style buildings of the Ostzeile. The historic Wertheim House (Haus Wertheym), the only building to have survived the 1944 air raids that destroyed much of old Frankfurt, can also still be seen and is now home to a popular restaurant. Built-in 1479, it's an undeniably romantic setting for a memorable meal.

Justice Fountain

Inside the Frankfurt Cathedral

The Städel Museum (Städelsches Kunstinstitut und Städtische Galerie), with its excellent collection of paintings from the 14th century, is the most important of the world-class museums that make up Frankfurt's Museum District (Museumsufer). Frankfurt's Museum District (Museumsufer) on the south and north banks of the River Main is a first-rate collection of some 16 separate museums, many of them of international standing. Located in the heart of Frankfurt's Inner City (Innenstadt) district, the 200-meter-tall Maintower (Aussichtspunkt Frankfurt) should rank highly on your list of fun things to do. Considered one of the top tourist attractions in Germany, it was completed in 1999, this impressive 56-story skyscraper is one of the largest in Germany and was built with a superb rooftop observatory that's open to the public. Located on Bockenheimer Landstrasse, the beautiful 54-acre Palm Garden (Palmengarten) is the largest botanic garden in Germany. One of three such gardens in Frankfurt, it was an instant hit with the public upon its opening in 1871. In fact, the attraction lured some of the top performers of the time from around the world, including Buffalo Bill, who visited with his Wild West show in 1890. When we visited the Palm Garden there were lovely outdoor botanical exhibits laid out according to their geographical location, along with several greenhouses containing subtropical and tropical plant species. The gardens also offer boating, a children's playground, and picnic spots, and guided tours are available. The Europaturm, a 337-meter-tall telecommunications tower also known as the "Tower of Europe," is just a short walk away and worth visiting for its viewing platform and restaurant. Great views can also be enjoyed from the viewing platforms of the nearby Main Tower, one of its tallest skyscrapers. The Roman Catholic Frankfurt Cathedral (Frankfurter Dom) certainly stands out for its lovely color. Officially known as St. Bartholomew's Cathedral (Dom St. Bartholomäus), its dazzling exterior comes from the red sandstone it was built with between the 13th and 15th centuries.

Inside the Palm Garden

The opera House

Add to this its Gothic styling and 95-meter-tall tower, and this impressive cathedral still manages to stand out in this city of skyscrapers. One of only a handful of churches in Germany to be designated as an Imperial Cathedral, it was here in the Election Chapel from 1562 to 1792 that the coronation of Emperors took place. Frankfurt was the birthplace of Germany's greatest writer, Johann Wolfgang von Goethe. His family home, Goethe House (Goethe Haus), was where Goethe was born on August 28, 1749, and lived until 1765. Immaculately preserved, it shows how the well-to-do family and their staff would have lived at the time.   The Eschenheim Tower

(Eschenheimer Turm) was built in the early 1400s and remains the finest relic from Frankfurt's old town walls. Standing 47 meters high, it still impresses with its dimensions and dominates the Eschenheimer Gate district. Situated in the heart of Frankfurt's Opera Square (Opernplatz), the Old Opera House (Alte Oper) was constructed in 1880 in the style of the Italian High Renaissance. Destroyed during World War II, it was rebuilt and reopened in 1981 as one of the city's most important concert venues. Fun English-language guided tours are available. After walking in the city centre and crossing the iron footbridge having a good view of the Main river, came back towards the Historisches museum, then towards Alte Nikolia Kirche, Frankfurt Cathedral. We could go inside the cathedral and observe the paintings and exhibits inside. Then we were in Frankfurt's Kleinmarkthalle which is a marketplace in the city centre. This area has a lot of tall buildings for which Frankfurt is famous.

Inside the Butterfly Garden

One of the towers in Frankfurt

We approached the Gothe House and the Opera House, Situated in the heart of Frankfurt's Opera Square (Opernplatz), the Old Opera House (Alte Oper) was constructed in 1880 in the style of the Italian High Renaissance. The Eschenheim Tower (Eschenheimer Turm) was built in the early 1400s and remains the finest relic from Frankfurt's old town walls. Walking through the city centre and enjoying the old and new buildings we again reached the Hapthwache and taking suitable U Bahn and S Bahn reached the Hotel. It was 8 PM. and therefore it was time to have dinner and take rest.

HEIDELBURG.

On 30th may 2024, Thursday, we had breakfast and reached Frankfurt HBF from where we used RB 68 to reach the beautiful city of Heidelburg. It is about 100 KM from Frankfurt and can be visited in a day. We met first a family from Mumbai who guided us regarding the things to see and how to use the local transport. Then we went to the Information centre from where we collected some more information and we were to go to the old city center and take a funicular to reach the castle.

The Heidelburg Castle

The Biggest barrel

We reached the Rathaus which is at the centre of the old town and from there we bought tickets for the funicular. When we were buying the tickets we met a family from Pune who stayed very close to our house in Pune. It was a Sathye family and Anagha Sathye had her residence in the same area as that we have our residence in Pune. We were with the family while going through the funicular. Anagha and her family were staying in Frankfurt and their senior family members were on a visit to Frankfurt. All of them had come by car from Frankfurt. We had a good discussion with them while going to the castle using the funicular. We reached the Elizabeth gate and viewed the towers and the old city from there. Then we went inside the Castle. The Celler contains a big barrel, which is called a big barrel because its size is the largest in the world. Then there is a beautiful observation tower and also a pharmacy museum dedicated to homeopathy. The display shows the process used to obtain the products, the materials used for that, and the final products. All of our Raw Indian Masala items are used for the synthesis.

The Pharmacy Museum

The Old Bridge

Nuremberg Castle (German: Nürnberger Burg) is a group of medieval fortified buildings on a sandstone ridge dominating the historical centre of Nuremberg in Bavaria, Germany. The castle, together with the city walls, is considered to be one of Europe's most formidable medieval fortifications. It represented the power and importance of the Holy Roman Empire and the outstanding role of the Imperial City of Nuremberg. Nuremberg Castle comprises three sections: the Imperial castle (Kaiserburg), the former Burgraves' castle (Burggrafenburg), and the buildings erected by the Imperial City at the eastern site (Reichsstädtische Bauten). The first fortified buildings appear to have been erected around 1000. Thereafter, three major construction periods may be distinguished, the castle built under the Salian kings respectively Holy Roman Emperors (1027–1125), a new castle built under the Hohenstaufen emperors (1138–1254), reconstruction of the Palas as well as various modifications and additions in the late medieval centuries. The usual access to the castle is via Burgstrasse ending in front of the sandstone ridge. A wide footpath leads into the outer courtyard through the Heavenly Gate (Himmelstor) situated next to the Hasenburg tower, named after the Bohemian Hasenburg family. The Sinwell Tower built in the 2nd half of the 13th century was the major keep of the Castle. It is named after its cylindrical form, in Middle High German sinwell means perfectly round. In the 1560s, its height was increased by a further floor and a pavilion roof with a pointed helm.

The Herb tower

The Statue at the Marktplatz

     The Deep Well (Tiefer Brunnen) inside the small half-timbered house in the middle of the courtyard is certainly as old as the castle itself, as it was the castle's only source of water. Its shaft reaches the water level at a depth of 50 meters (164 feet) and the water usually is 3 m (10 ft) deep. Above the water level, a niche was cut out of the rock for cleaning purposes. The lower stone walls of the building date from 1563. The little annex built in the following year was used as a bathroom and changing room. The Deep Well provided sufficient quantities of water for normal consumption, but during Imperial Diets and visits by the Emperor, water barrels had to be transported on wagons from the city. The Inner Gate, Inneres Tor, leads to the Inner Courtyard (Innerer Burghof), surrounded by the Palas, the Imperial Chapel , and the Kemenate. In the courtyard, remains of foundations of the Salian Period may be seen. In the middle, there is the Kunigunde Lime Tree planted in 1984, replacing older trees first mentioned in 1455 and named after Saint Cunigunde, consort of Emperor Henry II. The Palas, the main building of the Imperial Castle, has two floors which were used for official functions and as the Emperor's residence. It was rebuilt and modified a number of times during the castle's history. It now houses the permanent exhibition. The Burgraves' Castle was situated in the area between the Sinwell Tower and the Luginsland, but after its destruction in 1420 and the purchase of its remains by the city, very little was left. The Pentagonal Tower standing above the northern rock face is among the oldest buildings on the castle rock. It was the keep of the Burgraves' Castle. Its lower part made of ashlars may have been built at the same time as the Imperial Chapel. During later gothic times, a story of brickwork was added. The old town of Nuremberg absolutely deserves a good, leisurely stroll. There are beautiful houses at almost every corner, a lot of interesting churches to discover, and many pleasant spaces to rest. The White Tower, a gate tower of Nuremberg's penultimate city fortification, stands on Ludwigsplatz in the old town of Lorenzen. The Ehekaruessell is a fountain in the old town of Nuremberg and stands directly next to the White Tower. With the construction of the underground in Nuremberg, a ventilation shaft had to be created. To conceal this, the idea came up to build a fountain around the opening. The sculptor Jürgen Weber designed the fountain, which was erected in 1984. Not only the figurative depiction, which was partly considered vulgar but also the considerable budget overrun was a thorn in the side of the city's citizens and the fountain was highly controversial. The fountain shows six larger-than-life groups of figures that depict different scenes of a marriage, sometimes in a very drastic way. The basis for this is a poem by Hans Sachs. If you look at the hot-dip galvanized bronze statues, you will discover, for example, depictions of first love, marital strife, and death. The Nassau House is opposite the Lorenzkirche. It is the only tower house that still exists in Nuremberg and one of its most famous buildings. It stands out between all the half-timber houses. The tower is made of red sandstone. The tower was probably never used for defense. The alcoves and the armorial rim are particularly eye-catching. Nuremberg is the hometown of Albrecht Dürer and in many places all over the city, one can find his   traces.

He was a painter, drawer, and graphic designer, he wrote pieces on proportion theory, geometry, and fortification. Dürer's "Praying Hands" and "Young Hare" are his most reproduced pieces. The Unschlittplatz with the Unschlitthaus is located in the southern part of Nuremberg's Old Town. The square is one of the city's most important medieval sights. The Unschlitthaus gave the square its name. The impressive building was erected by the city in the 15th century as a granary. In 1562, the Unschlittamt was established on the ground floor. Until 1835, all butchers had to bring the waste fat, the so-called Unschlitt, here and sell it to the town. Unschlitt was an important raw material for the production of tallow candles, wagon grease, and shoe polish until the 19th century. The Frauenkirche, Church of our Lady is on the Central Market Square. It is one of the most important churches of the city. It was supposed to hold the imperial regalia such as the emperor's crown, coat, and sceptre but that never happened. The Church of Our Lady is the first Gothic hall church in Franconia. In the old town of Nuremberg, there is a fountain on the Hauptmarkt called the "Schöner Brunnen". With this information available we were in the castle and after seeing the museum we walked towards the Herb Tower and then in the garden to see Neptune Brunnen. Since there was a possibility of rain we chose to take the funicular to reach the Rathaus and then the Karlsplatz.

Church of holy Spirit　　　　　　　The entrance of the Old Bridge

This area is in the famous University area. This is a very old university. Passing through the small streets we reached the Old Bridge. On the way, we could see the church of the holy spirit. The old bridge is on the Naker River. The river is a mode of transport and we could see the vessels passing along. After visiting these places we used the bus to reach the HBF and then the Train to reach Frankfurt. From the HBF we reached the hotel. This was our second last day of the tour.

On the last day, we were supposed to go for dinner at Puneet Iyer's house and meet Anita and Gundu whom we had met on the first day after landing at Frankfurt. Instead of S Bahn we chose the bus just next to our hotel and reached the Frankfurt Sud HBF. Luckily we had a few stores to buy some things that we would carry to our house. Also, the tram which reaches Puneet's house also had its starting point at this place itself. Taking tram No 16 we reached the city centre and since we had sufficient time we planned to see the Palm Garden. It is located on Bockenheimer Landstrasse, the beautiful 54-acre Palm Garden (Palmengarten) is the largest botanic garden in Germany. We have to buy a ticket to enter the garden. The first part is the rose garden. There are a large variety of roses in the garden. Then there are different greenhouse gardens, the cactus, the South American, the African, and many more. Finally, we went to the butterfly garden. The garden was actually under maintenance but we could see a variety of butterflies. The entire garden took around 3 hours to see and then it was time to reach the Puneet Iyer's house. We reached there, had our dinner, the discussions regarding our visit to various destinations and then taking the S Bahn we returned to the hotel. The next day we checked out from the hotel and took a bus to reach the Frankfurt Airport. After taking the boarding pass and handing over the luggage, we were in our boarding area. The flight was on time and also reached on time to Mumbai from where we had the Star air flight to Kolhapur. We reached Kolhapur at 10.30 A.M. and our Home. Thus our 21-day Germany visit was completed. We enjoyed the tour and with an intention to make use of the planning process, I am preparing this write-up. It was a well-organized trip and I must not forget to thank the organizing committee of the tour under the leadership of Mr Randeep Todkar from the Samarth holidays, Kolhapur.

The text depicted in this write-up may be useful for any traveller who wishes to tour Germany and visit the places mentioned.

www.ingramcontent.com/pod-product-compliance
Lightning Source LLC
Chambersburg PA
CBHW040148110726
48005CB00018B/2688